"I'm Tony Meisner. What can I do for you?"

Was she a relative of someone they had previously rescued? Very occasionally someone like that stopped by to say thank you.

"I'm Kelsey Chapman." She stared at him intently.

The name jolted him. "Elizabeth Chapman," he said, without thinking.

The flash of pain in her eyes told him he had guessed right. "She was my sister. I didn't know if anyone would remember her after so much time."

"I remember," Tony said.

"You remember her?" Kelsey said.

All these years he had wondered if anyone would ever show up, asking about Liz. She had come to town alone, and she had died alone, but he had never believed a person so full of sweetness hadn't had someone, somewhere, who loved her. The woman standing in front of him now looked enough like Liz he could almost imagine they were standing together in the hallway at the high school after class.

"I was there," he said. "I knew Liz before she disappeared. And I was the one who found her."

KILLER ON KESTREL TRAIL

CINDI MYERS

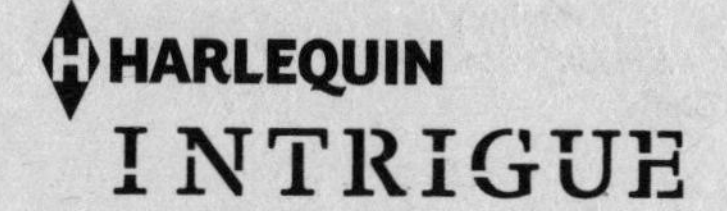

For Gini.

Recycling programs for this product may not exist in your area.

ISBN-13: 978-1-335-59050-3

Killer on Kestrel Trail

For questions and comments about the quality of this book, please contact us at CustomerService@Harlequin.com.

Harlequin Enterprises ULC
22 Adelaide St. West, 41st Floor
Toronto, Ontario M5H 4E3, Canada
www.Harlequin.com

Printed in U.S.A.

Cindi Myers is the author of more than seventy-five novels. When she's not plotting new romance story lines, she enjoys skiing, gardening, cooking, crafting and daydreaming. A lover of small-town life, she lives with her husband and two spoiled dogs in the Colorado mountains.

Books by Cindi Myers

Harlequin Intrigue

Eagle Mountain: Critical Response

Deception at Dixon Pass
Pursuit at Panther Point
Killer on Kestrel Trail

Eagle Mountain Search and Rescue

Eagle Mountain Cliffhanger
Canyon Kidnapping
Mountain Terror
Close Call in Colorado

Eagle Mountain: Search for Suspects

Disappearance at Dakota Ridge
Conspiracy in the Rockies
Missing at Full Moon Mine
Grizzly Creek Standoff

The Ranger Brigade: Rocky Mountain Manhunt

Investigation in Black Canyon
Mountain of Evidence
Mountain Investigation
Presumed Deadly

Visit the Author Profile page at Harlequin.com.

CAST OF CHARACTERS

Kelsey Chapman—Kelsey was only eight when her sister left home, but she has come to Eagle Mountain hoping to learn the truth about her death.

Tony Meisner—Tony knew Liz during the brief time she lived in Eagle Mountain and was the one who discovered her body. Twenty years later, that discovery still haunts him, and he wants to help her sister find closure.

Liz Chapman—Twenty years ago, this strong-willed eighteen-year-old left her home in Iowa to move to Colorado to be with a man she had met online. She was found dead a few months later and her murderer has never been found.

Mountain Man—Liz moved to Eagle Mountain, Colorado, after meeting a mysterious man online, whom she only referred to as Mountain Man. Kelsey believes finding him is the key to solving her sister's murder.

Ted Carruthers—Ted was captain of Eagle Mountain Search and Rescue when Liz was found and oversaw the recovery of her body. He doesn't think any good will come of Kelsey's investigation.

Chapter One

Tony Meisner gritted his teeth against the pain in his leg and focused on getting down the trail. Hot sun beat down on the back of his neck; he wished he could stop and shed the blue Eagle Mountain Search and Rescue parka he was wearing. He had needed the coat on the shady side of the mountain, but here in the early-April sun, he was hot in spite of patches of snow on the ground. Carrying one corner of a stretcher with a one-hundred-eighty-pound man aboard was proving how out of shape he was after months off-duty.

But he was still mobile, he reminded himself—unlike the poor guy he was helping to carry on the litter. The hiker had fallen when a section of Kestrel Trail broke loose, and he sustained a closed fracture in his right leg. Thanks to Eagle Mountain Search and Rescue, he was on his way to a waiting medical helicopter. With time and therapy, he would hike again in a few months.

"And here's our relief," Danny Irwin called out as a quartet of SAR volunteers appeared over the next rise.

Tony tried not to groan as he lowered his corner of the litter and volunteers Eldon Ramsey, Ryan Welch, Carrie Andrews and Grace Whitlock moved in to carry their patient for the last leg to the helicopter-landing zone.

Tony pulled a bottle of water from his pack and eased onto a rock. "How are you doing?" Medical officer Hannah Richards, whose day job was a paramedic, sent him a concerned look.

"I'm fine," Tony said. He rubbed his hands down his thighs, both of which had sustained fractures in a climbing fall last year. The pain didn't matter, because he knew every day would be a little better. He could have waited a few more months to return to duty, but he had needed to be back with Search and Rescue where he belonged.

Caleb Garrison, a new volunteer with the group, settled beside Tony on the rock. "I understand you've been with SAR a long time," he said.

"Since I was seventeen, and I'm thirty-eight now," Tony said. He stowed his water bottle. Caleb was twenty-five. Tony was a SAR veteran at that age. He had a wealth of experience now, but he tried to stay open to the possibility of always learning more.

"You don't get burned-out?" Caleb gestured down the trail, in the direction the other volunteers had headed. "You must have seen some pretty intense stuff."

Tony nodded. He had responded to suicides, drownings, fatal falls and more than one mission that had gone from rescue to body recovery in a matter of minutes. "I guess this work is part of my DNA now," he said. "I missed it while I was out."

"Not many high school kids would be interested in doing this, I wouldn't think," Caleb said.

"We require all our volunteers to be eighteen now, but when I started, there wasn't an age limit," Tony said. He had been new in town, lost and lonely. Eagle Mountain Search and Rescue had welcomed him and given him a new family. He owed them more than he could ever repay.

He looked around and realized with a start that he and Caleb were sitting almost exactly where one of his first rescues had taken place. "I had only been with the group a few weeks when we found the body of a missing young woman right here," he said.

"No kidding?" Caleb said. "What happened to her?"

Tony shook his head. "We never found out. A teacher reported her missing a little over a week before. The medical examiner ruled she had been strangled, but I don't think the person who did it was ever found." He shrugged. "Thankfully, we don't get that kind of call very often. All of our missions don't have happy endings, but we usually have a good idea of exactly what happened." The *knowing* was a kind of closure. At the end of the day, a good mission might mean being confident they had done everything they could to help the person they'd been called to save.

"How many calls do you think you've been on all these years?" Caleb asked.

"A couple of thousand?" Tony guessed. In the early days, they might get one call a month. Now, with increased tourism and more people drawn to outdoor adventures, they might respond to half a dozen calls a month. Tony hadn't responded to all of them, but he had been part of the team for most and captain three different times.

"I'm amazed you remember a call that happened so long ago," Caleb said.

"You know what they say," Danny, who had been listening, chimed in. He winked and smirked at Tony. "You never forget your first."

"I remember them all," Tony said. Every mission was seared on his memory—what the weather was like, who had participated, the challenges they had overcome, and whether or not their patient had survived.

"Did you ever think about not coming back to SAR after your accident?" Caleb asked.

"Never." Through the long days in the hospital and during his time in a rehabilitation facility—and the hours and hours of difficult and sometimes excruciating physical therapy—the prospect of returning to search and rescue work had sustained him and kept him going. Every time they responded to a call, SAR volunteers had the chance to make a difference—for the people whose lives they attempted to save and for their families. "We do this work for other people," Tony said. "But we do it for ourselves, too. Because it fills some space inside of us. At least, it does for me." Everyone wasn't as dedicated to Eagle Mountain SAR as he was. Maybe that meant they didn't need it to complete them the way he did.

Sometimes the memories of the rescues that hadn't ended well weighed on him, but most of the time he was proud to have made a difference. So little else in his life had.

KELSEY CHAPMAN HAD never been west of Mount Vernon, Iowa, when she steered her Honda

Civic down the main street of Eagle Mountain, Colorado, on a bright Tuesday morning in early April. She slowed the car to a crawl and almost stopped in the middle of the street as she stared up at the snow-covered mountains surrounding the town. *This* was the place Liz had described as "the most beautiful spot in the world." Now Kelsey finally knew what her sister had meant.

She forced her gaze back to the street until she spotted the sign ahead for the Alpiner Inn. Some of the tension went out of her shoulders as she pulled the car into an angled spot right in front of the inn. She had made the reservation online not knowing what to expect, but the place looked nice—a sort of Swiss Alps vibe, with fancy wood trim on the eaves and shutters, and window boxes awaiting flowers. She paused for a second on the sidewalk to gaze at the mountains again. Liz had been up there somewhere. All these years, Kelsey had wondered what had happened to her sister, and now she was finally going to find out. It hardly seemed real.

Her cell phone vibrated; she pulled it out of her pocket, glanced at the screen and then answered. "Hi, Mom. I just pulled up in front of my hotel here in Eagle Mountain."

"So you haven't found out anything yet?" Mary Chapman sounded out of breath, as she too often was these days.

"Are you using your oxygen, Mom?" Kelsey asked.

"I'm fine."

"The doctor said you needed to use it if you got short of breath."

"I don't like dragging that machine around. And I'm just excited, that's all. What is Eagle Mountain like?"

"It's very pretty." Looking down the street literally meant looking *down*, as the elevation fell from one end of the town to the other. "Lots of Victorian buildings, cute little shops and restaurants, and snow-covered mountains in the distance. Like a postcard."

"I'll never think of that place as anything but ugly," Mary said.

A little of Kelsey's excitement over being here drained away. "Now that I'm here, I understand a little better what Liz loved about it."

"Find out what happened to her," Mary said. "That's all I care about."

"I'll call you tomorrow," Kelsey said. "Maybe I'll know more by then, but it might take longer than a couple of days."

"Someone must know something," Mary said. "I tried to persuade your father to hire a private detective to go down there right after it happened, but he wouldn't hear of it."

"Dad wanted to pretend Liz never existed," Kelsey said.

"Don't be too hard on your father," Mary said. "Losing Liz broke his heart. He couldn't talk about her because it hurt too much. And he felt guilty, too. The two of them said some ugly things before she left."

"You would think he would want to know who killed his daughter," Kelsey said.

"I think he felt better not knowing," Mary said. "You don't understand that now, but someday, when you have children, you might."

They said goodbye, and Kelsey pulled her roller bag from the back of the Civic and trundled it inside the lobby. A blonde close to Kelsey's age looked up as she entered. "Hello," she said. "What can I do for you?"

"I'm Kelsey Chapman. I reserved a room for two weeks." She didn't know if that was enough time for what she needed to do, but she had to start somewhere.

"Welcome to Eagle Mountain. I'm Hannah, and my parents, Brit and Thad, own the inn. If you need anything while you're here, let one of us know."

Kelsey handed over her credit card and waited while Hannah processed the charge. The inn had what Kelsey imagined was Scandinavian decor—lots of pale wood and blue and white cushions, antique ice skates, and skis and sleds on the wall, in addition to many framed photos of the surrounding mountains. "Are you here on business or pleasure?" Hannah asked as she returned Kelsey's credit card.

"Um, just vacationing," Kelsey said. Certainly no one was paying her to be here, but she couldn't consider her task a pleasurable one, either.

"There's lots to see and do around here," Hannah said. "Let me know if there's anything in particular you're interested in. And definitely check with me before you go hiking. Some of the trails higher up still have too much snow on them to attempt just yet. I don't want to have to bring you back to town on a stretcher."

At Kelsey's alarmed look, Hannah laughed. "Sorry. I volunteer with Search and Rescue. Plus, my main job is as a paramedic. I've seen so many accidents I tend to want to warn everyone who is new around here."

Kelsey's heartbeat sped up. "How long have you been with Search and Rescue?" she asked.

"Six years."

Not long enough, Kelsey thought. "Do you have volunteers who have been with the group longer?" she asked.

"Oh, sure. We've got one member who has been with the group almost twenty-one years."

"What's his—or her—name?" Kelsey asked.

Hannah looked amused. "Why are you so interested?"

Kelsey could have spilled the whole story then and there, but she was afraid people might dismiss her as a kook. "I'm always interested in people's stories," she said. "If I run into someone who's volunteered to save other people for twenty-one years, I want to know their name."

"It's Tony," Hannah said. "And you'll know when you see him because he's probably wearing a Search and Rescue T-shirt or hoodie. I think that's his whole wardrobe." She leaned closer, her tone confiding. "But seriously, don't let all this search and rescue talk make you think this is a dangerous place."

This is *a dangerous place*, Kelsey thought, but she only smiled as she accepted her room key from Hannah. *My sister died here*, she could have said. *And I'm trying to find out who killed her.*

TONY STAPLED THE last of the handouts for the training session he was teaching Tuesday evening on dealing with head injuries and added it to the stack at the end of the folding table. The power point equipment was hooked up and functioning. He had added a few new photographs from last week's rescue up on Kestrel

Trail. The man they had rescued was at St. Joseph's in Junction and expected to make a full recovery.

A beep indicated a door had opened, and he turned to see a young woman with long dark brown hair leaning around the door. "Hello?" she called, tentative.

"Hello." Tony walked forward to meet her. He had been making more of an effort not to limp, and he thought the practice was paying off. His goal was to get back to his previous level of fitness, no matter how long it took. "What can I do for you?" he asked.

"I'm looking for Tony." She smiled, and he felt a tightness in his chest. She was beautiful, with straight hair almost to her waist; blue, blue eyes; and a slender yet decidedly feminine figure. She was also young—ten or even fifteen years younger than he was, which made him feel a little like a dirty old man.

"I'm Tony Meisner. What can I do for you?" Was she a relative of someone they had previously rescued? Occasionally someone like that would stop by to say thank you.

"I'm Kelsey Chapman." She stared at him intently.

The name jolted him. "Elizabeth Chapman," he said without thinking.

The flash of pain in her eyes told him he had

guessed right. "Yes," she said. "But everyone called her Liz." Her expression softened. "She was my sister. I didn't know if anyone would remember her after so much time."

"I remember," Tony said.

"You remember…finding her?" Kelsey said. "Someone told me you were with Search and Rescue back then. Were you there the day…the day they found her…her body?"

All these years, he had wondered if anyone would ever show up asking about Liz. She had come to town alone, and she had died alone, but he had never believed a person so full of sweetness hadn't had someone, somewhere, who loved her. The woman standing in front of him now looked enough like Liz that he could almost imagine they were standing together in the hallway at the high school, after class. "I was there," he said. "I knew Liz before she disappeared. And I was the one who found her."

Chapter Two

Wanting to make the most of her time in Eagle Mountain, Kelsey had stayed at the Alpiner only long enough to drop her luggage and freshen up. She had driven through town, trying to get a feel for the place and hoping to figure out where to begin her search. When she'd spotted the sign for Eagle Mountain Search and Rescue headquarters, she took a chance someone would be there who would know Tony Meisner or another veteran volunteer who could fill in some of the details about Liz's death. She hadn't expected to get this lucky.

When she thought about the Search and Rescue team who had located Liz's body and carried her down a mountain into town, she had pictured a bunch of buff, young guys. Lifeguards in ski jackets, maybe. But Tony Meisner had silver streaks in his thinning blond hair and even more gray in his neatly trimmed goatee. He had fine lines at the corners of his blue eyes, as if he had spent a lot of time squinting into the sun. The skin of his face was weathered, too, like someone who had lived a life outdoors. It was a nice face, though; one she liked looking at. Not movie-star handsome but attractive. And it was a kind face. One Liz would have liked.

Then the full impact of his words hit her. "You knew Liz?" she asked. "Before she died?" *Before she was murdered.* It was such a hard thing to say.

"She and I were the same age," Tony said. "We went to the same high school. Well, the only high school in Eagle Mountain." He raked a hand back through his hair. He had big hands, with long fingers, and a trio of colored rubber bracelets around his wrist. "She was one of the popular kids. One of the beautiful girls. I didn't have the nerve to speak to her." He half smiled, his expression rueful. "I just admired her from afar."

"You had a crush on her."

His cheeks burned. "I guess so."

"Lots of guys had crushes on Liz." Their home phone had rung constantly with calls from boys wanting to speak to Kelsey's pretty, older sister. After Liz had left, the silence made them that much more aware of her absence.

"You must have been pretty young when she went missing," Tony said.

"I was eight. But I remember sitting on the end of her bed, watching her at her dressing table while she got ready for a date. She had so many boyfriends, and I thought she was the most beautiful girl in the world." Her expression sobered. "If you knew her, you must have recognized her right away when you found her?"

AND NOW CAME the questions. He understood. People wanted to know what had happened to their loved ones, as if knowing all the details might help them understand the tragedy better, help them accept it more easily—though Tony didn't believe that was ever the case. He checked his watch. He still had an hour before the other volunteers were likely to start showing up. "Why don't you take your coat off and sit down," he said. "I'll get us some coffee and try to answer your questions."

He retreated to the tiny galley kitchen that had been installed when Search and Rescue had constructed these "new" headquarters ten years before. By the time he returned to the front of the building with two cups of coffee, Kelsey had shed her coat and settled into a folding chair near the front of the room.

Tony took the chair beside her and passed over one of the cups of coffee. He held out a handful of creamer and sugar packets. "Thanks." She plucked out a packet of sugar but didn't immediately add it to her drink. Instead, she studied him until he began to feel uncomfortable.

"What is it?" he asked.

"I'm trying to picture you at eighteen," Kelsey said. "That's really young to be working search and rescue, isn't it?"

"Actually, I was seventeen. Maybe too young, but nobody thought about that in the day," he said. No one had worried he would be scarred by the tragedies he had seen, and no one had tried to shield him from the sight of dead or mangled bodies. He thought he had handled things as well as could be expected but was aware not everyone would agree.

She sprinkled the sugar into her coffee and stirred. He sipped his own drink and sat back in the chair. "What do you want to know?" he asked.

He braced himself for the usual questions: How was she found? What did she look like? Did she suffer? What happened to her?

But that's not what Kelsey asked. "Do you think she was happy here? Before she was killed, I mean?"

An image popped into his head. Liz Chapman, in low-rise jeans and a pink tank top that rode up to show off a gold hoop in her navel, leaning back against the stone wall outside

Rocky Top Ice Cream, laughing. The sun always seemed to shine on people like Liz, and others had gravitated to her. She had been popular but also genuinely nice. "I think she was happy," he said. "Or as happy as any teenager ever is."

Kelsey smiled. "I do remember the angst of high school." She rested her chin in her hand. "Did she ever talk about her home back in Iowa?" she asked. "About us?"

"I'm sorry," he said. "I didn't know her that well. I didn't even know until later that she wasn't living with her family here in town. I don't think I had ever met a high school student who was just…on her own."

"Not exactly on her own," Kelsey said. "She was living with a guy. Did you know him?"

He frowned. "I didn't know she was seeing anyone in particular." She had flirted with several guys at school, though he couldn't remember her dating anyone. Their senior class had been small—eighteen people. Everyone knew everything about everyone else, or so they had thought. After she died, they'd learned Liz had a lot of secrets.

Kelsey sipped her coffee. "Liz met a guy online. I don't know his name. The only thing my mom could remember was that he signed his emails 'Mountain Man.' He was supposedly twenty-one and lived in Eagle Mountain, Colorado. Liz said he had a good job and he wanted her to come live with him. She was eighteen, so my parents couldn't really stop her." She looked into her coffee. "I used to wonder sometimes how hard they tried. Does that sound awful?"

He shook his head. Then, because she still wasn't looking up at him, he said, "No. But some parents keep a tighter hold on their children than others." His own had kept almost no hold at all, happy to have him drift away from their responsibility.

Kelsey nodded but didn't seem inclined to continue the conversation. He wanted her to keep talking, so he picked up where she had left off. "I heard there was a guy the sheriff's department was looking for after she died," he said.

"Then why didn't they find him?" Her voice rose with agitation. "I looked online, and this is a small town—only about fifteen hundred people. And it was even smaller back then. How could someone not know this guy?"

"I don't think anyone at school knew she was living with a boyfriend," Tony said. "She was just another teenage girl, and she acted like one. She flirted with the popular guys and hung out with the other cool kids. I never saw her with an older guy."

Kelsey nodded. "That's what the police told my mother—that no one in town knew Liz was living with an older man. My mom said the cop who called practically accused her of making up the whole story. Or maybe there was no boyfriend and Liz lied to our parents about why she wanted to leave. But if that was true, how was she supporting herself? She didn't have any money saved up, and the cops said she didn't even have a part-time job after school. She had to be living somewhere and eating regular meals."

"Do they think the boyfriend killed her?"

"That seems the most likely thing, doesn't it?" Kelsey said. "Especially since he disappeared after she died. Mom said the police never even found Liz's belongings—just the items she had in her locker at school. She took two suitcases with her when she left home, and we don't have any idea what happened to them." She leaned toward him. "What did people in town say about her? Surely there was gossip."

"All I heard was that everyone was shocked that she was here on her own, without her family," he said. "People were worried some random serial killer had come to town. Things like this didn't happen in Eagle Mountain back then. Before Liz was killed, I don't think there had been a murder here in thirty years."

"Had Liz made any enemies while she was here?" Kelsey asked. "Were there any suspects at all?"

"I don't know," he said. "A few months after she was found, I graduated and left for a summer job with a white water raft company in Montana, and college after that, so I lost track of what happened." By the time he had moved back to town, no one was talking about Liz anymore.

"My dad was so angry after Liz left that he couldn't stand for anyone to even mention her name. My mom tried to stay in touch, but Liz didn't have a cell phone. Not many people did back then. I know Mom sent a few letters in the mail, but they came back unopened."

"That must have been hard." He thought about his own family, who hadn't really kept in touch with him, for different reasons. "Do your parents know you're here now?" he asked.

"My mom does. My dad died last year." She traced a finger around the rim of her coffee mug. "After he was gone, my mom started talking about Liz again. Mom has COPD and couldn't make this trip, but I think she's happy I decided to come." Her eyes met his, the blue of lake water, sad but not despairing. "We can't bring Liz back, but we'd still like to know what happened."

He nodded. "Of course you would. I would, too."

Kelsey pushed the half-full cup of coffee away. "I think I'm ready now," she said. "Tell me about when you found her."

Twenty years ago

TONY TOLD HIMSELF he would run all the way to the top of the trail, then allow himself to walk part of the way down. He had to get in better shape if he was going to keep up on search and rescue calls in the mountains. He was pretty tall—over six feet already, and he would probably add a couple more inches by the time he stopped growing. But he was too scrawny. His sweat-soaked T-shirt clung to his torso, showing the outline of his ribs. He had started lifting weights, but his brother had already complained Tony was eating him out of house and home. He tried to fill up at the restaurant where he worked after school, where one meal was included as part of his pay, but lately, he was always hungry.

He pushed himself to keep pounding up the trail, though he had a stitch in his side and his lungs hurt. He could do this. He wiped sweat from his eyes and squinted into the sun. Just a few more yards. One foot in front of the other.

Whomp! He fell hard, knees stinging when they hit the ground. He swore and rolled over, one hand shielding his eyes from the sun. He lay there panting, trying to catch his breath, then slowly sat up and looked around. At least no one else was around to see him. He leaned over and rubbed his left knee, which was bleeding a little. He felt his ankle. It seemed okay. With a grunt, he pushed himself up.

Then he looked around for whatever had tripped him. Something white lay in the middle of the trail. White and pink. At first he thought it was a deer bone. A leg, maybe. He leaned over for a closer look, and something about the arrangement of bone and ligament sent a shudder through him. Heart pounding, he searched near the trail. To the right of the trail, up a small rise, something fluttered. Like a scarf floating in the breeze.

He hiked up toward it. Not a scarf. Hair, long and brown—a silk banner lifted by the wind.

He didn't recognize Liz Chapman right away. Death distorts the features, and animals had found her before he did. But something about the body was so familiar that he forced himself to look closer. He thought it might be Liz. Those same low-rise jeans, with the rip above the left knee. She had had this little gold chain with a heart pendant that she wore around her neck, but he didn't see it now. A pack rat or crow might have claimed such a treasure. He remembered those details from too many hours of watching Liz when she didn't know he was looking at her.

And everyone knew Liz was missing. There had been an article in the paper, and kids talked about it at school.

Tony closed his eyes, surprised to feel tears. Then he turned and began running again. Back down the trail and toward town.

"THEY TOLD US she had been strangled," Kelsey said, her voice bringing Tony back to the present and the quiet of the Search and Rescue building.

"I couldn't tell you anything about that," he said. He set his coffee cup aside and leaned forward, elbows on his knees. "When a body has been exposed to the elements, that takes a toll. And we have a lot of wild animals up here, too. I'm not trying to upset you—just trying to explain why it's hard to tell much just by looking."

She swallowed and nodded, but he knew she didn't really understand. He hadn't, until he had seen Liz. Later, there had been others: People ejected from motor vehicles. Fallen climbers. Skiers caught in avalanches. Fishermen who'd drowned. Every death horrible in its own way. The only comfort for him was knowing the person hadn't felt anything after their last breath. They didn't care what happened to their body after that.

"Was there anything about her body or the scene that struck you as unusual?" she asked.

"No." Not that death was ever ordinary, especially a violent death in the middle of nowhere. But he thought he knew what she meant. Had he seen anything that stood out, that might provide a clue as to what had happened to her? He shook his head. "There was nothing." The place where she had lain had been quiet and peaceful. "When I found her, I thought she must have fallen and hit her head," he said. "I was shocked to find out she had been murdered."

"I'd like to see where you found her," Kelsey said.

He nodded. "I can take you." Kestrel Trail was a pretty spot, one he had visited many times since—most recently when rescuing the fallen hiker. Liz had died there so long ago that there was nothing left to indicate her passing. Going there might help Kelsey find a little peace.

Chapter Three

Kelsey's friend Amber had suggested Kelsey begin her search at the Eagle Mountain newspaper. "Small town papers keep back issues," Amber, who had majored in journalism at the university where she and Kelsey had been roommates, had said. "You should be able to find the issues around the time your sister disappeared. And the local library probably has the high school yearbooks. You could check those for any pictures of her while she was there."

Part of Kelsey's mission here was to try to reconstruct what Liz's life had been like, in hopes of discovering how that had led to her murder, and to try to understand what was here that had led Liz to leave them all behind. On her second morning in Eagle Mountain, Kelsey went to the offices of the *Eagle Mountain Examiner.* A woman with a cascade of blonde corkscrew curls looked up from a desk as Kelsey entered. "May I help you?"

"I'm looking for some back issues of the paper," Kelsey said. "From twenty years ago."

The woman slid out of her chair and moved from behind the desk. "I'm Tammy Patterson," she said, and extended a hand.

"Kelsey Chapman." They shook, and Kelsey was sure Tammy was taking in every detail, from her scuffed flats to her wind-blown hair.

"What dates of the paper are you looking for?" Tammy asked.

She gave her the information, anticipating just what Tammy would be able to unearth in the archives.

"Come through here to our morgue," Tammy said. "Let's see what we can find."

She led the way to a small room lined floor to ceiling with shelves that supported oversize scrapbooks full of past issues of the paper. Tammy pulled out a ladder, climbed it and started passing down volumes to Kelsey. "Each one of these books has six months of the paper," Tammy said. "We came out twice a week back then. Now we're just a weekly."

Kelsey deposited each volume on the table behind her before turning to accept the next. Tammy climbed down and dusted off her hands. "Is there something in particular you're looking for?" she asked.

"My sister disappeared from Eagle Mountain

twenty years ago last May," she said. "Her body was found a little over a week later."

"I'm so sorry." Tammy rested a gentle hand on Kelsey's shoulder.

"Thanks. I just want to know as much as I can about what happened."

"Of course. Take as much time as you need. And if you want copies of anything, I can help you with that, too."

Left alone, Kelsey opened the first volume. She was two weeks into the month before she found the first story. "Local Woman Missing," declared the headline, with a photograph of Liz, one Kelsey hadn't seen before. She leaned closer, the musty odor of newsprint filling her nose as she studied the grainy image. Liz stood in a group of other girls, in what must have been a school gymnasium. She wore shorts and a T-shirt that read Lady Eagles on the front, and knee pads. What sport was she playing? Volleyball, maybe?

Liz's image had been singled out and enlarged, but her features were blurred. She was a pretty, young girl with a big smile, her hair pulled back in a ponytail. She looked younger than Kelsey remembered. Less glamorous when seen from Kelsey's adult perspective. Much too young to be on her own in the world.

Kelsey read the article, which reported that

one of Liz's teachers had contacted the sheriff's department after being unable to reach Liz and finding that the address she had given on her school records was a vacant apartment. "Elizabeth Chapman, 18, moved to Eagle Mountain in late March of this year and enrolled in the local high school as a senior," the article continued. "When contacted in Ms. Chapman's hometown of Mount Vernon, Iowa, her father, Reginald Chapman, stated that his daughter had left home of her own accord shortly after her 18th birthday and the family had not been in contact with her since."

Kelsey turned the page, and glanced over ads for a video-rental place, a bowling alley and the local grocery store. The paper carried high school sports scores, horoscopes and an article about plans for the upcoming senior prom.

The next issue of the *Examiner* contained another article about Liz, this one without a picture. "Law enforcement officials are searching for information about a man Elizabeth Chapman may have been dating and possibly living with when she disappeared," the article reported. "Her family in Iowa know this man only as Mountain Man, from emails he sent to Elizabeth before she left Iowa. Students at Eagle Mountain High who knew her say she never mentioned a male friend or talked about her living arrangements. 'We figured she lived with her parents, like the rest of us,' said Jessica Stringfellow, a teammate of Elizabeth's on the Lady Eagles volleyball team."

The third issue Kelsey opened contained papers from the first two weeks in May. Almost immediately, Liz's photo jumped out at Kelsey. Not the blurry school photograph but the professional shot taken at the beginning of Liz's senior year, before she left home. A coy smile on her lips, one hand tucked under her chin, Liz looked directly into the camera—a pretty, fresh-faced brunette, with a look of such confidence in her eyes it made Kelsey catch her breath. This picture had hung in the hallway of their home for several months after Liz left, until one day, Kelsey had come home from school to find it gone, along with every other photograph of her sister.

"Your father burned them all," her mother had told her shortly after her father's funeral. "He said it hurt too much to see them."

Kelsey would get a copy of this article and send it to her mom. At least she would have this one photo of her eldest daughter.

The article that accompanied the photo told of the discovery of remains near Kestrel Trail that were suspected to be those of Elizabeth Chapman, eighteen, who had disappeared approximately eight days before, after having run away from her home in Iowa to Eagle Mountain, supposedly to live with a man who had not been identified or located.

The article was continued on a second page, where Kelsey found a photograph of a young Tony Meisner, shaggy blond hair falling over his eyes, smooth faced and bony shouldered. His eyes were the same: pale hazel and sadder than anyone that young should be.

Two more articles after that reported that Liz appeared to have been strangled, probably very close to the time she disappeared. No one had come forward with information about Mountain Man, and her personal belongings, beyond the few items collected from her locker at the high school, had never been found.

Smaller articles over the coming weeks reported on the failure to locate the mysterious Mountain Man and the disappearance of Liz's personal belongings. Some students had organized a candlelight vigil for her at a local park. Kelsey studied the picture of the event—a cluster of girls and a few boys holding candles and looking solemn. Was one of the people in this photo the person who had killed her? Her gaze focused on a tall, skinny boy at the edge of the crowd, a mop of blond hair falling into his eyes, and she smiled. Tony looked so young and awkward in this photo, so different from the strong, capable man he appeared to be today. Yet this boy had the same light eyes, their expression shy and slightly troubled.

And then there was nothing else. No more updates or photos. Everyone had forgotten about Liz Chapman. Everyone except her family and Tony Meisner. Kelsey could tell from the way he had described finding Liz's body that he had never forgotten.

TONY HAD ARRANGED to pick up Kelsey from the Alpiner Inn Wednesday afternoon at five, after he got off work at Eagle Surveying. He had been in the field all day, and he came straight to the inn in his usual uniform of khaki hiking pants and an Eagle Mountain Search and Rescue T-shirt. "Hey, Tony," Hannah greeted him as he entered the lobby of the inn.

"Hello, Hannah."

Hannah's dad, Thad Richards, emerged from a back room. "Hi, Tony," he said. "You're looking fully recovered. Are you climbing again yet?"

"Starting to," he said. His doctors had cautioned him not to attempt much yet, but he was beginning with some easy ascents and descents.

"Did you need something from me?" Hannah asked.

"Actually, I'm here to see Kelsey."

Hannah didn't even try to hide her surprise. "Kelsey Chapman?"

"Hi, Tony. Sorry I kept you waiting." Kelsey came into the lobby and saved him from having to respond to Hannah—who apparently found the idea of a man like Tony with a woman like Kelsey incredulous.

Kelsey looked ready for a hike, in jeans and a long-sleeved T-shirt and hiking boots. She carried a day pack in one hand. "See you later," she said, and waved to Thad and Hannah.

"Are we in a hurry?" she called after Tony as he rushed across the parking lot.

He stopped and waited for her to catch up. "Sorry," he said. "I tend to walk fast." Really, he had just wanted to get away from Hannah's and Thad's stares.

He opened the passenger door of his truck, and Kelsey tossed in her pack, then climbed in after it. She was buckling her seat belt by the time he slid behind the wheel. "Thanks for doing this," she said.

"No problem. It's a beautiful day for a hike." He inserted the key and started the engine.

"I spent the morning at the newspaper office," she said. "I read some articles about Liz that were printed at the time of her disappearance. They talked about a place called Kestrel Trail?"

"That's where we're headed."

"Is it very far up in the mountains?" she asked.

"Not too far. A couple of miles."

"I'm just trying to figure out what Liz was doing up there. We don't have mountains—or really that much hiking—in Iowa."

"Hiking is really popular here," he said. "There are so many beautiful places to go."

"So her killer might have suggested they take a hike and then, when they were all alone, he strangled her?" She grimaced.

He thought about how to answer. "It could have happened that way," he said after a moment. "Even though the trails are popular, it's possible to spend a whole day hiking and never see anyone else. But I don't know if the sheriff's department believed she was killed where she was found. I never heard."

She swiveled toward him. "Do they think she was killed somewhere else and brought to that location?"

"I don't know." Liz had looked almost peaceful when he found her but also unreal—more like a mannequin than a once-living person. "You should talk to someone at the sheriff's department. Maybe they'll let you see their files." He glanced at her. "If you're sure you really want that much detail."

"I want detail." She faced forward again. "I want to find Mountain Man. Someone must have seen him or knows who he is, even if they never connected him to Liz."

"I'm sure local law enforcement looked hard for him," Tony said.

"I read a lot of other articles in the paper while I was looking for news about Liz," Kelsey said. "I found out that the Rayford County Sheriff's Department in 2002 had only three full-time deputies and the sheriff. And two of the officers and the sheriff were convicted of drug trafficking only two months after you found Liz's body. So I don't think they looked that hard for her killer at all."

He remembered hearing about that scandal now, though he had been away during that time. "The current sheriff isn't like that," he said. "Maybe he'll try to help you."

She turned toward him again. "You went away to school, but you came back here to live," she said. "How long were you away?"

"A little over two years." Long enough to get his associates degree and his license as a surveyor. He had landed a job with Eagle Surveying, signed back on with Search and Rescue, and hadn't left since.

"Do a lot of people do that? Come back here after they graduate?"

"Some do. Quite a few, I guess." He could name a dozen of his classmates who still lived in town. "There are a lot of people here who went to school with Liz, if that's what you're getting at."

"Could you introduce me to some of them?" she asked.

"I could do that." He wondered how much they would remember. Had Liz made as much of an impression on them as she had on him?

They reached the trail head and got out. Kelsey slipped on her pack, then turned in a slow circle, looking up at the surrounding mountain peaks. "This really is gorgeous," she said.

"In another month, most of the snow will be melted and the meadows will be carpeted with wildflowers," he said. "I'm sorry you'll miss it." She hadn't said how long she intended to stay in Eagle Mountain, but she probably had a job and family and friends to go back to.

"It's still beautiful," she said.

He led the way up the trail, careful to keep his steps slower. Behind him, he could hear her breathing hard. It always took a few weeks for people from other places to adjust to the altitude. "Tell me if I'm walking too fast," he said.

"You're fine." She moved in closer. "Have you lived in Eagle Mountain all your life?"

"No. I moved here the year before Liz." In a

small town where most of the students had been together since preschool, he had been the "new kid" until Liz had shown up.

She didn't respond right away, but he could sense her waiting for him to elaborate. She was expecting to hear about his family moving to town for work or because they had vacationed here and loved it. "I came to live with my brother," he said. "He was sixteen years older than me."

"Oh." Another long pause. "Did something happen to your parents?"

Something *had* happened. "They got tired of raising me." He glanced at her, trying to read her expression behind her dark sunglasses but unable to do so. Still, she didn't make any noises that sounded like pity. "I was a surprise baby. Way later than my brother. My mom made no secret of the fact that she was horrified when she got the news that she was pregnant with me. The summer I turned sixteen, she sent me to stay with my brother. At the end of the summer, she informed me that she and Dad felt it would be better for everyone if I stayed here. Then they sold the house and moved to Arizona."

"Wow," Kelsey said. "How did your brother react?"

"He tried to be nice about it. He said he was happy to have me here, but who is really happy to take in a teenager? Especially an unhappy teenager?"

"I saw your picture in the paper. You were cute."

"I was a skinny, awkward kid—too shy to string two sentences together."

"How did you get involved with Search and Rescue?"

The tension in his shoulders eased. Here was something he was more comfortable talking about. "I saw a poster at school, about a program to be a junior SAR volunteer. The idea was to get young people interested in the work. Me and one other kid showed up to the first meeting. I was the only one who came back for the second. Rather than run a program for one person, they decided to treat me like any other volunteer, and I started training. Nobody there seemed to care that I was from someplace else or too quiet or awkward. They treated me like everyone else and made me feel like I wasn't a total loser. I could make a difference." He glanced at her again. "And now you know way more about me than you want to."

She hooked her thumbs beneath the straps of her pack. "You and I have more in common than I thought," she said.

"How is that?"

"My parents didn't move away or send me to

live with a relative when I was in high school. But they might as well have. After Liz died, it was as if every bit of life went out of our house. They were so wrapped up in guilt and grief I might not have even existed. They stopped caring about anything. It felt like they stopped caring about me."

He heard the pain in her voice and felt it in his chest—that pain of being abandoned. When he had first come to Eagle Mountain, his brand-new driver's license told him he was almost an adult. He ought to have been able to take care of himself. But inside, he'd felt like a little boy, wanting to cry out for his mother but not daring to do so. "I'm sorry," he said. "That's rough."

"I didn't just miss my parents," she said. "I missed Liz, too. She was ten years older than me, but she never acted like I was in the way. She liked hanging out with me and was always taking me with her and playing with me. If I got scared in the middle of the night, I would crawl into her bed, not my parents'." She paused, head down as she walked up the trail. Tony said nothing, knowing that sometimes silence offered the greatest comfort.

"The night before she left, she came to my room and gave me a present," Kelsey continued after a moment. "It was a little gold necklace with a heart. She had one just like it. She said she wasn't ever going to take off her necklace, because it reminded her of me. She had to go away for a little while, but she would come back to see me soon. She would bring Mountain Man with her so I could meet him, and she knew I would like him as much as she did.

"I cried and begged her not to leave me, but she said she had to." Her voice broke, and she cleared her throat. "She said when you loved someone, you wanted to be with them—and as much as she loved me, she needed to be with him right now."

"She called him 'Mountain Man' when she was talking to you?" Tony asked. "Not his name?"

"She said he had asked her not to use his real name."

"Do you think it's possible she didn't *know* his real name?" Tony asked.

"I don't know. I've thought about it a lot over the years, and I wondered if he wasn't some serial killer who lured young women over the internet, then murdered them. I used to go online and look for similar crimes, but I never found any."

"What did she tell you about him?" Tony asked. "I've been trying to think of all the men I knew in town then. Maybe I knew this guy and didn't even realize it."

"She said he was twenty-one, he was good-looking, and he had a good job and his own apartment in Eagle Mountain, Colorado."

"'Good-looking' how?"

"She didn't say. And I didn't ask. I mean, I was eight years old. I thought *good-looking* meant he looked like an actor on television."

He laughed in spite of himself, and she laughed too. The sound was like tension being released from a spring. "I'm hoping she confided more in someone here," she said. "Maybe a girlfriend she was close to."

"I'll find some people for you to meet," he said. "I want to help."

He stopped at the top of a rise and looked around, orienting himself. The air was still and hushed, with green grass showing between patches of melting snow and clouds scudding along in a cerulean sky. "Is this the place?" Kelsey asked, her voice quiet.

"This is where I found the first bone." He pointed to the trail beneath their feet. "The rest of her was up there, on that little ledge." He started out, picking his way around snow and across rock until he came to the place. For a moment, he imagined he saw her there, her long hair floating on the breeze; his mind was playing tricks on him.

Kelsey stared at the site for a long time, not

saying anything, then looked up at him. "Were you afraid?" she asked.

He blinked. "No. I wasn't afraid. Just…sad."

"Sad because she was your friend?"

"Yes. And sad because I couldn't help her."

"It was too late for you to rescue her."

He nodded. He hadn't thought about it like that, but he supposed that was true.

"How far have we hiked up the trail?" Kelsey asked.

"A little over two miles."

"So you had a long way to run for help that day. And a long way to carry the body down after that."

"Not so far in search and rescue terms. Some days we travel a lot farther, and not on defined trails."

"It still seems such a remote place for Liz to come with her killer." She shook her head. "And I can't see someone hauling a dead body all the way up here."

"Is there anything else you'd like to see while we're here?" he asked.

"No. I'm ready to leave. Thank you for bringing me up here." She hooked her arm through his and leaned against him. "I wish you had known her better," she said. "I think she would have liked you."

He wasn't so sure about that. The Liz he had

known was one of those girls who were aware of the power of their beauty. She hadn't been cruel, but she was oblivious to the feelings of those outside her immediate circle. She might have noticed Tony, but only to assess that he wasn't someone she needed to be concerned about. He'd moved outside of her orbit. It was probably the way he struck most people. He had a lot of friends in Eagle Mountain, but he wasn't really close to anyone. He didn't let that bother him. Some people were loners, and he was one of them.

Chapter Four

Kelsey had never been inside a police station before—or, in this case, a sheriff's department. She steeled herself to have to plead to see her sister's case file; she was determined to make the best argument possible to be allowed access. But instead of the brusque desk sergeant she had imagined—possibly from watching too many crime shows—at the Rayford County Sheriff's Department, she was greeted by a pleasant older woman with a cap of white hair, blue-rimmed glasses and earrings in the shape of dragonflies. "How can I help you?" the woman, whose name tag identified her as Adelaide, asked.

"My name is Kelsey Chapman, and my sister, Elizabeth, was murdered here over twenty years ago," she said. "The case was never solved, and I would like to see her case file."

Adelaide nodded. "Let me find someone to speak with you," she said, and disappeared through a door.

While she waited, Kelsey studied the photographs on the walls of the small waiting area. Men and women in khaki uniforms posed for the camera, in groups and alone. One prominent photo showed a very handsome dark-haired man looking into the camera lens with a solemn, determined expression.

"Sheriff Walker will see you now," Adelaide said. She led Kelsey down a short hallway to an office, and the man in the photo, who was even better looking in person.

"Travis Walker," he introduced himself with a firm handshake.

Kelsey sat across from him, and he lowered himself into his leather desk chair. "Your sister was Elizabeth Chapman?" he asked.

Kelsey nodded.

"You must have been very young when she left home."

"I was eight."

"Why are you looking into her death now?" he asked.

Kelsey told herself she should have anticipated this question. Her first instinct was to reply "Because she was my sister," but she expected the sheriff wanted more. "My parents refused to talk about what happened when I was growing up," she said. "After my father died, my mother opened up a little more, but she couldn't tell me much. I really think I need to know the details, to put together a picture of what happened here." She leaned forward, gripping the edge of the desk. "There was a big age difference between me and my sister, but I loved her very much. I believe she loved me."

"I've asked someone to retrieve the file for you," the sheriff said. "When I took over as sheriff, I reviewed all our cold case files, so I'm familiar with your sister's case. There are some things in there that would be difficult for most people to see. When Elizabeth's body was found, it had been exposed to the elements for a number of days."

"I'm aware." She wet her dry lips. "I've spoken with Tony Meisner."

"The photos are in a separate envelope within the file. You don't have to view them if you don't want to."

Kelsey didn't want to, but she felt she needed to. She nodded.

"No one on the force now was part of the sheriff's department back then," Travis said. "The force was much smaller at that time, and there were problems with corruption."

"I saw some articles in the paper," she said, "when I was researching Liz's murder."

Travis's mouth tightened. "I'm not making excuses for them. The case is still considered open—and if, after reviewing the file, you believe you have new information that can help locate her killer, I want to hear it."

"Of course."

"Also, if you have questions about anything in the file, I or one of my deputies will do our best to answer them. Sometimes the things we do in the course of an investigation don't make sense to civilians."

"Thank you." What else could she say? She hadn't expected it to be so easy to get the information they had collected about Liz's death.

A knock on the door interrupted them, and a big, blond deputy came in and set a trio of cardboard file boxes on the desk. Kelsey's eyes widened. "There's more than I expected," she said.

"This doesn't include the physical and DNA evidence," the sheriff said. "That's stored at a separate facility. But there are descriptions in the case files."

"You have DNA evidence?"

"Yes. We've run it through the state and national databases and attempted matches a couple of times but have never come up with anything."

"So if you had a good suspect, you could take a sample of his DNA, and if it matched, you would know you had the killer?"

"Yes," the sheriff said. "If you're aware of

someone we should take a closer look at, be sure to let us know."

"I will." She had a lot of questions about Liz and what had happened to her, but she wanted to wait until after she read the file to see what information she could glean from there.

The sheriff stood, and she rose also. "Deputy Ellis will show you to a room where you can look through these. Take your time, and if you need anything, let us know."

The blond deputy picked up the file boxes again and led the way to a small, windowless gray room with a single table and chair. A box of tissues sat in the middle of the table. "The ladies' room is at the end of the hall on the right, and there's a watercooler right outside the door," he said as he set the boxes on the table. "Can I get you some coffee or anything else?"

"No thank you." She laid a hand on top of the boxes. "I appreciate your help."

He nodded. "I'm sorry for your loss." Then he left the room and closed the door behind him.

Kelsey settled in the chair. It wasn't particularly comfortable, but she wasn't here to be comfortable. She wondered if this was a room where they interviewed suspects. Overhead, the round eye of a camera was focused on the table. There was probably a microphone, too. Was she being recorded right now? If so, it was going to be a very boring tape.

She set her purse on the floor beside her chair and removed her jacket, then lifted the lid on the first box. Her initial impression was of many thin pieces of paper shoved into file folders. Most of the papers were forms, with many lines of typed or handwritten narrative. It took a moment to orientate herself. The first piece of paper was the initial missing person report, filed by a woman named Deborah Raymond, identified as an English Literature teacher at Eagle Mountain High School. She had stated that Liz had failed to attend classes for the past three days. None of her friends had reported seeing her. Ms. Raymond had visited the home address in Elizabeth's school records and found a vacant apartment. She'd spoken with a neighbor, who had told her no one had lived in the apartment for months. The woman hadn't known Liz.

Subsequent papers included reports of interviews with other teachers, Liz's friends and the owner of the empty apartment, who reported the rental had been unoccupied since the first of the year. Liz had never lived there.

She studied the names of the friends: Madison Gruenwald, Jessica Stringfellow, Marcus White, Ben Everett, Sally d'Orio. None of them had known what had happened to Liz. All of them had seemed surprised to learn that she didn't live with her mother and father. School administrators had reported that Liz had enrolled with all the proper paperwork, including transcripts from the school she had attended in Iowa. None of the people questioned had ever met Liz's parents, but since the enrollment forms had been properly signed, administrators hadn't been alarmed.

Finally, there was a record of a telephone interview with Kelsey's mother and father, who had only reported that Liz left home after she'd turned eighteen; there was no mention in this report of Mountain Man.

Fascinated, Kelsey kept reading and began to take notes, writing down the names of everyone the sheriff's department had interviewed and any information she hadn't known before. Two weeks after Liz was reported missing, Kelsey found the first mention of Mountain Man. A follow-up interview with Mr. and Mrs. Chapman, conducted by a sheriff's deputy in Iowa on behalf of the Rayford County Sheriff's Department, had revealed Liz's online relationship with someone who'd signed off on his emails as "Mountain Man." He and Liz had met on an internet chat board for the band Phish, then began a long correspondence.

Kelsey turned the page and stared at printouts of some of these conversations, apparently printed from the Chapman-family computer:

MountainMan *MountainMan@hotmail.com*
To: *RealLiz@iowanet.com*
Subject: Life Together

Parents always have a hard time letting their chicks leave the nest, but you're a grown woman and you know your own mind. It's one of the things I love about you. Can't wait to have you here with me. I want to show you the mountains. I want to be a real lover to you, not just on paper. Let me know when you're ready and I'll send you the bus tickets.

RealLiz *RealLiz@iowanet.com*
To: *MountainMan@hotmail.com*
Subject: Re: Life Together

I'm ready! Send the tickets. I am getting everything together here. I can't believe how easy it was to get everything I needed from school. I walked into the vice principal's office and told him I was moving to Colorado and needed my transcripts and stuff to enroll in school there and he printed out everything right then, no questions asked. I haven't told anyone else (except the parents, who are in denial. They're pretending I'm not going to go through with this, but I am!)

MountainMan *MountainMan@hotmail.com*
To: *RealLiz@iowanet.com*
Subject: Re: Life Together

I'm so proud of you, Babe. You are going to love it here. Look for the tickets in the mail ASAP. Remember what we talked about—don't give your folks any way to find us, in case they get it into their heads to try to keep you from doing what you've decided to do. After you're settled here you can send them your new address but for now, let's keep it a secret.

RealLiz *RealLiz@iowanet.com*
To: *MountainMan@hotmail.com*
Subject: Ready or Not, Here I Come

Got the tickets and my bags are packed. I am so ready. Big fight with the parents last night. I thought Pop was going to stroke out. But I'm 18 and he can't stop me. The hardest part is leaving little Kelsey behind. But we'll get her out for a visit as soon as we can—maybe this summer. She's a cool kid—I know you'll like her.

Three days and counting til I see you. Can't wait! Hugs and kisses, Liz.

Kelsey blinked back tears and reached for the tissue box. Hearing Liz describe her as a "cool kid" made a lump swell in her throat that threatened to overwhelm her. She got up and fetched water from the cooler in the hall. *Keep it together*, she told herself. She still had a long way to go.

She returned to the files. The next folder contained correspondence with Hotmail and Iowanet, trying to discover the identity of Mountain Man, but this led nowhere. Hotmail verified that the account originated in Eagle Mountain, Colorado, yet could not provide a name, address or any other information about the account holder. But a handwritten scrawl at the bottom of one page noted that the Mountain Man account had been closed on February 14—the day Liz arrived in Eagle Mountain.

There was a gap in the paperwork after that. For more than a month, nothing was added to the file. Then another flurry of reports, dated May 23. First up was Tony's statement about finding the body. It included everything he had told her—clearly the details hadn't faded with time. There were statements from the deputies who'd responded to the scene and the coroner's autopsy report.

Kelsey hesitated before reading this last, then plunged in. The clinical language was distancing, making it easier to absorb the information without really relating it to her sister. The victim had been a Caucasian female, aged seventeen to thirty; brown hair, blue eyes; five feet, seven inches tall; approximately 125 pounds. Her remains had been found by a hiker midmorning on May 23.

A detailed description of the physical examination and findings followed, but the salient points for Kelsey were that Liz had died of strangulation approximately two weeks before the remains were found. She had no other significant injuries, though broken fingernails and skin cells recovered from beneath her fingernails indicated she had struggled with her attacker. There was no evidence of sexual assault or recent sexual activity. No indication of illegal or prescription drug use was found. The skin cells underneath her fingernails had been collected for a possible DNA match to any suspects.

Kelsey closed her eyes and thought for a moment of her sister struggling with her killer. Liz had been young and fit. Maybe a woman could have overpowered her, but her killer was probably a man. She liked men and always had at least one trailing after her. She had come to Eagle Mountain to meet her Mountain Man. And with her last breath, she had fought with her killer, collecting the evidence beneath her fingernails that might one day be used to convict him.

It has to be Mountain Man, Kelsey thought. If he wasn't the killer, why hadn't he come forward to report that Liz was missing? If he had really loved her, he would have been frantic, wouldn't he?

But if he had killed her, he would want to make sure no one knew he existed.

Someone must know. Eagle Mountain was a small town. All she needed was to find one person who knew about Mountain Man. Then the sheriff could test for a DNA match.

The first file box was almost empty now. A thick brown envelope labeled Crime Scene Photos lay at the bottom. Kelsey fished it out and weighed it in her hand. Did she really want to see these?

She did not, but what if she—the person who knew her sister better than any of these dispassionate investigators—spotted something at the scene that could lead to the killer? It was probably a fantasy, thinking she would arrive and miraculously solve the crime, but she couldn't let go of the idea.

She took a deep breath and slid the stack of photos out from the file.

The first photo wasn't too shocking—a distant view taken from the trail of the area where the body lay. Various people stood around the area Kelsey recognized as the bench where she had stood with Tony.

Subsequent photos moved in closer, like a slow-motion movie. When she finally arrived at the body, it was so unlike the live Liz that at first it was like looking at a doll or some other inanimate object—limbs sprawled, hair trailing. Nothing about the image suggested the lively, loving girl Liz had been.

Next came a series of close-ups of the body. Kelsey skimmed these, rapidly shuffling through them. She wasn't going to see anything here except the stuff of nightmares.

She paused when she reached a series of photos of the scene. Apparently, these were items found on the ground near the body—a cigarette butt, a ruler laid beside it to show that the size was two centimeters long. A note on the back indicated the brand of cigarette. A tube of lip balm and a single gum wrapper received similar treatment.

Next came photos taken indoors: A pair of

women's jeans, size four, a small rip above the left knee. A pink long-sleeved blouse, ruffles at the wrists. Three gold hoops—a pair of earrings and a navel ring.

Kelsey stilled and reached up to finger the necklace she was wearing. She had rarely taken off the small gold heart on a gold chain since Liz had given it to her over twenty years before. Liz had one just like it, and Kelsey couldn't remember seeing her sister without it since she had received it as a gift from their grandmother on her sixteenth birthday. She gripped the heart and stared at all that was left of her sister. "What happened to you?" she whispered.

THURSDAY AFTER WORK, Tony hit the gym. He did a few stretches to warm up, then grabbed a pair of twenty-pound dumbbells and set up for lunges. Left side. Right side. He concentrated on keeping the proper form, not leaning forward. His recently mended legs protested at the strain, and the surgery scars down both legs glowed white against his flushed skin. After ten reps, he rested, sweat beading on his forehead. Then he did another ten. And another.

He sat on the weight bench for bicep curls, muscles bulging. He was still tall and thin but no longer skinny. Hours of climbing had sculpted the muscles of his back, chest and arms. He didn't lift out of vanity—who was he going to impress? But strength might save his life one day, or the life of someone else.

"Hey, Tony."

He looked up and smiled as Ted Carruthers dropped his towel onto the bench next to Tony's. Ted was one of the founders of Eagle Mountain Search and Rescue. He had been captain the year Tony joined and had served as the younger man's mentor. Retired now in his midsixties, Ted still served as the group's historian and was writing a book about some of their most exciting rescues. "How's it going, Ted?"

"Days like this, I think I retired too soon," Ted said. He sat on the bench and began pulling on elastic knee braces. "I'm still in better shape than most guys half my age."

Tony said nothing. Ted had been pressured to retire from search and rescue work after a series of mistakes and bad choices that had endangered his fellow volunteers and the people they served. Ted was a good guy, but he let ego get in the way of good sense sometimes. Having him as historian—still available to consult, if necessary—was a better fit for the group these days. No one had a better understanding of local topography than Ted, who had lived and worked in the area for forty years.

"I heard everyone came down without a

scratch off Mount Baker the other day," Ted said, referring to the rescue SAR had made of a skier who had been trapped in a couloir.

"Everything went smooth as butter," Tony agreed. He resumed curling the weight, moving slowly and deliberately.

"Anything new with SAR?" Ted selected a dumbbell and lay back for a series of chest presses.

"Do you remember that girl who went missing not long after I joined SAR—Elizabeth Chapman?"

Ted sat up. "What made you think of her?" he asked.

"Her sister is in town. Younger sister. She was only eight when Elizabeth—she calls her Liz—left home. She's trying to find out what happened and came to me because she heard I'd found the body. But you were captain then. You probably remember more than I do."

Ted lay back down again and resumed exercising. "Why would she want to bring all that up again after twenty years?" he asked.

"They never found out who killed her sister," Tony said. "I guess she just wants to know more of the story."

"Not much to tell," Ted said. "We found her body up on that mountainside. No clues. We'll probably never know what happened."

"Still, I think Kelsey would like to talk to you."

Ted grunted, thrusting the weights. He lowered them and turned his head to look at Tony. "What's the sister like?"

"She looks a lot like Liz." The Liz he remembered from high school.

"What does she do when she's not digging up the past?"

"I don't know. I didn't ask her."

Ted snorted. "I bet you don't know anything else about her, do you?"

He knew that she had felt abandoned by her family, the way he had. He knew she had loved her sister and felt close to her in spite of their age difference. He knew he felt comfortable with her, something he didn't feel with most people. "We talked about her sister," he said.

"It's just as well you're a bachelor," Ted said. "You would drive a woman up the wall."

"Says a man who's never been married himself."

"Never married, but I've had plenty of women in my life. You might not believe it now, but I was quite the stud in my day."

Tony bit the inside of his mouth to keep from laughing at the use of the word *stud*. He did have memories of the younger Ted escorting various women around town, several of them married to other people. He had long suspected the older man liked women he wouldn't have to commit to. "Will you talk to Kelsey Chapman?" he asked.

"Sure, I'll talk to her." He sat up again. "I can't tell her any more than you did. Probably less since I didn't know that girl while she was alive. But if she wants to know how Search and Rescue operated back in the day, I'm happy to bore her with all the details."

"Great. I'll tell her." It would give him an excuse to talk to Kelsey again. The thought was a nice distraction from the pain of working out.

Chapter Five

Kelsey had set aside the second file box and was preparing to start on the third when someone knocked on the door of the little room. She looked up to see Sheriff Walker. "How's it going?" he asked.

"I'm learning a lot," she said. She looked at the notes she had made. "I think the killer had to be Mountain Man."

Sheriff Walker leaned against the door frame, arms crossed. "What do you know about him?"

"Not much. Liz never used his real name. She told us he was in his early twenties, had his own place and a good job. She didn't say what kind of work he did. She never described him, except to say he was good-looking." She shook her head. "I can't believe no one who knew Liz had heard of him."

"He apparently wanted her to keep their relationship secret."

"Why?"

"Maybe he was married. Maybe he was older than he had told her. There could be a lot of reasons. She may have thought it was exciting or romantic, sneaking around."

"She might have. Mom always said Liz loved drama."

He nodded toward the file boxes. "Is there anything else in there that stood out for you?"

"Liz's necklace is missing." She pulled out her heart necklace again. "Like this. She had one like it, and she never took it off. But I didn't see it listed in the description of her clothing and jewelry."

He leaned forward to study the gold heart. "I'll double-check the evidence locker, but if she was wearing that when she was found, it would have been listed. There were problems with the department back then, but it looks as if they did a thorough investigation."

"Yes," she agreed. "They talked to everyone who knew Liz, even a little bit. But they still couldn't find out who killed her."

"There's no statute of limitations on murder," the sheriff said. "If we find any new information, we'll investigate it."

She nodded. "Thank you."

He straightened. "Take as much time as you like. If you have any more questions, come to my office or ask someone to find me."

"Thank you."

He left, and she prepared to examine the last box, which seemed to include follow-up interviews. She hadn't gotten far when another knock interrupted her. The door opened and Adelaide entered, a to-go cup in one hand, a paper bag in the other. "I brought you some lunch," she said. She set the bag and cup on the table, then took a chair from the corner and moved it across from Kelsey and sat. "And I thought I'd keep you company while you ate. Give you a break from all this." She nodded at the case files. "It can be pretty grim, reading cold case files."

"You've done it?" she asked. She popped the lid on the cup and saw a tea bag floating in hot water. Not her favorite, but she wouldn't be picky. The sandwich was chicken, which *was* her favorite. "You didn't have to bring me lunch," she added.

"You need to eat," Adelaide said, and Kelsey smiled.

"To answer your question, yes, I've looked through case files before," Adelaide said. "My husband was a police officer, then a detective, in Cleveland for many years before we retired to Eagle Mountain. After he passed, I was bored silly. I applied for an opening for an office manager here at the sheriff's department, and I've been here ever since."

"Were you here when my sister disappeared?" Kelsey asked.

"No. But I know the stories you've probably heard about the sheriff's department back then." She met Kelsey's gaze, her expression stern. "I want you to know the men and women here now aren't like that. Sheriff Walker is a straight arrow. A good man, and every deputy he hires is the same. If they weren't, they wouldn't be here. If you find any information about your sister's killer, you can trust them with it. You can trust them to do the right thing."

Kelsey nodded and chewed a bite of sandwich. After she swallowed, she said, "I know the department didn't have the best reputation back then, but from what I'm reading, they did a pretty thorough investigation. They collected a lot of evidence, and they interviewed lots of people who knew Liz. There just isn't much to go on. Liz supposedly came to Eagle Mountain to be with a guy she called Mountain Man. No one here has heard of him, and I can't find anyone who knew his real name or who even saw him with Liz."

"Could she have made him up?"

Kelsey sipped her tea. "She could have. But I never knew her to lie before. And there are lots of emails between her and this guy, and he sent her bus tickets to get from Iowa to Eagle Mountain. It would be a pretty elaborate ruse for her to go to the trouble to make all that up. And how would she have even heard of Eagle Mountain all the way back in Iowa?"

"So the guy was probably real, just very cagey," Adelaide said. "He probably told her not to tell anyone who he was. He would have made it sound mysterious and romantic. Some girls really like that sort of thing."

"Liz liked that sort of thing," Kelsey said. "My dad used to tease her, when they were still getting along, about being a drama queen."

Adelaide nodded. "You weren't the drama queen type, I'm thinking."

Kelsey looked down at the table. "I guess I figured my parents had suffered enough," she said. She had been a quiet kid—too quiet, really. She did well in school and went straight home afterward, the loss of her sister like a shield wrapped around her, keeping everyone else at bay. No one else could understand what she had been through, so why even try to make friends?

Later, in college, she had opened up a little more. She had joined several groups on campus, played tennis and started dating. But she had never gotten really close to anyone. She wasn't sure she ever could.

A phone rang and Adelaide pulled a handset from her pocket. "I'll leave you to your lunch," she said. "Remember, if it gets too overwhelming, you can always come back tomorrow. Those records have sat in those boxes twenty years. They can wait for you a day longer."

She left the room, the door closing softly behind her. Kelsey rewrapped the rest of the sandwich and set it aside, then reached for the next folder in the next box. Liz had waited a long time for justice. Kelsey didn't want her to have to wait even one day more.

THE DAY AFTER his meeting with Kelsey, Tony came home from work to find an unfamiliar motorcycle occupying the space where he usually parked his truck. A young man with blond hair to his shoulders and ragged jeans moved out of the shade of the arbor at one end of the front deck as Tony walked up from the street. "Hey, Uncle Tony," he called. "Long time no see."

Tony stopped and stared. "Chris?" he asked, taking a closer look at his brother's youngest boy. Chris had been three when Tony moved out of his brother's home and left for college, and Tony had seen him only sporadically in the twenty years since.

"The one and only." Chris held his arms wide,

then walked over to Tony and enveloped him in a rib-crushing hug. They were the same height and had the same thin frame, though Chris was less muscular and still had a bit of a baby face.

"What are you doing here?" Tony asked when Chris finally released him.

"I thought maybe I could stay with you for a while." Chris smiled, but Tony read doubt in his hazel eyes.

"So you just decided to come all the way from Denver for a visit?"

"Yeah, well… Mom and Dad sort of kicked me out."

Tony's stomach knotted. "What happened?"

Chris looked up at the sky. "I remember he took you in when you were a little younger than me, so I figured you could return the favor."

"Why did your parents kick you out?" Tony asked again.

Chris stared at the ground and scratched the back of his neck. "I got in a little trouble—borrowed a friend's car and sort of wrecked it."

"'*Sort of* wrecked it'?"

"Yeah, well, I smashed it up pretty good. But it wasn't my fault. A deer ran out in front of me, and I swerved to avoid it and hit a tree."

Tony nodded. This sounded like exactly the sort of thing Chris—whom his brother had described more than once as "irresponsible"—

would do. "I guess your friend was pretty upset."

"Yeah, especially since I hadn't exactly asked before I took the car. I thought I could have it back to his place before he even knew it was missing."

"Why aren't you in jail?"

"It was my first offense." Chris grinned. "Well, the first time I ever got caught. And I talked to the friend and pointed out his insurance would pay for the damage, so he agreed not to press charges if I would leave town for a while." He held his arms wide once more. "So I decided to come visit you."

Tony didn't know whether to be flattered or fearful of this declaration. "Did your mom and dad really kick you out, or not?" he asked.

"Well, they agreed I needed to leave town for a while, so when I suggested I come see you, they thought it was a good idea."

Tony had lived alone a long time, and the thought of having a roommate held no appeal. "I only have one bedroom," he said.

"No problem. I'll crash on the couch. I took a peek in the window, and it looks pretty comfy."

Tony wanted to say no. He didn't need this kind of complication in his life. But he still had a memory of two-year-old Chris climbing into his lap and falling asleep—maybe the first person who had ever trusted him so completely. "You'll have to get a job," he said.

"Yeah, sure. This is a tourist town, right? I'll find work at a restaurant or something."

"And no more borrowing cars. Or my truck." He looked back at his truck, parked at the curb. "And you need to move your bike out of my parking space."

"Sure. No problem. So can I stay?"

"You can stay. But only for a few weeks."

That grin again. The little boy shining through the almost-man. "Thanks!" He slapped Tony on the back. "We're going to have a great time. You'll see."

BY THE TIME Kelsey left the sheriff's department late Thursday afternoon, she felt as if her head was gripped in a vise and her shoulders ached with tension. Her mind was a jumble of visions and facts, from the images of Liz's body lying on that rocky mountainside to details about her last meal—a chicken sandwich and fries consumed five hours before she'd been killed. She knew more about her sister's life here in Eagle Mountain and subsequent death than she ever had before, but all the new information only blurred the picture of what had happened to end Liz's life more than ever.

Back at the Alpiner, she lay back on the bed,

eyes closed, and tried to clear her head. She must have drifted off, because the buzzing of her phone on the bedside table jolted her awake. She sat up and grabbed the phone, seeing her mother's number on the display.

"Hi, Mom," she said. "How are you?"

"Have you found out anything yet?" Mom asked. No *how are you* or *you sound tired* or anything like that. Mary always got straight to the point.

"I spent most of the day at the sheriff's department," Kelsey said. She lay back on the bed again, phone to her ear. "I read through the case file on Liz's murder."

"And?"

"It looks like they worked hard investigating the case," Kelsey said. "They talked to a lot of people and gathered a lot of evidence."

"But they didn't find Liz's killer, did they?"

"No," Kelsey admitted.

"Then they must have missed something. Did they even learn who Mountain Man was?"

"No. Apparently, Liz gave the school a fake address, and her friends all thought she lived with her parents."

"I thought everyone knew everything about everybody in small towns," her mother said. "Who were the primary suspects?"

"There weren't any," Kelsey said.

"That's ridiculous. They must have been suspicious of someone."

"There wasn't anyone, Mom."

"Then you need to find someone," her mother said. "That's why I paid for you to make this trip."

Kelsey winced. Her mother had paid for the room at the Alpiner for two weeks, her contribution to this fact-finding mission. Kelsey hadn't wanted to accept, knowing that her mother's gifts always came with strings. But she wouldn't have been able to afford to stay here without her mother's contribution, so she had kept silent. Now it was her turn to pay. "There's a lot to sort through," she said. "But I'm working hard to put everything together. I'm hoping I'll see or uncover something the investigators missed before."

"I hope so, too," her mother said. "Call me when you have news."

"Wait, Mom. How are you—" But Mary had already hung up.

Kelsey dropped the phone on the bed and closed her eyes again. A line from the report about the law enforcement interview with her parents came to mind: *Parents are upset but unable or unwilling to supply much information.*

That was her parents in a nutshell. Always

holding back, afraid of giving away too much, whether it was facts or affection.

TONY WAITED UNTIL Chris had gone "to check out the town" to call his brother, Eddie—he went by Edward now. He answered on the second ring. "I figured I was going to hear from you soon," he said. "I take it Chris showed up in one piece?"

"Was it your idea for him to come stay with me?" Tony asked.

"He had to go somewhere," Eddie said. When Tony didn't respond right away, he sighed. "Look, he's not a bad kid, he just doesn't think. It doesn't help that his friends here are as clueless and unmotivated as he is. Paula and I figured it would do him good to get away for a while, make a fresh start. And he might listen to you more than he does us. Make him get a job, help out around your place, whatever you think will straighten him out."

"I don't know anything about raising a kid—much less one who's already twenty years old."

"At his age, you and I were men," Eddie said. "We had to be. Chris still has some growing up to do. And he doesn't need another parent. He just needs a good example."

Tony almost laughed. "You think I'm a good example?"

"You own your own home, are gainfully employed in a good profession and you're involved in that wilderness-rescue stuff. And Chris has always idolized you. The two of you are a lot alike, you know."

Warmth spread through Tony's chest. "He hardly knows me," he said. "How can he idolize me?"

"He talks about you all the time, and he reads about you online, in that little paper Eagle Mountain has—all your search and rescue exploits. You gave us all a scare when you were hurt last year."

Eddie had made the five-hour drive from Denver to visit Tony in the hospital after he was out of ICU, but Chris hadn't come with him. "He wanted to come see you in the hospital," Eddie said. "I wouldn't let him, because I thought it would be too upsetting to see you like that, all banged up."

"You spoil him," Tony said without thinking.

"I wanted him to have a better childhood than you or I had," Eddie said. "Maybe I went a little overboard sometimes, but I'm not apologizing."

"I never said you should," Tony said. "I'll try to look after him while he's here. I told him he needs to get a job, and he said he would."

"That's a great start," Eddie said. "And if you need any money or anything…"

"No," Tony said. "I'm good."

"Well...thanks. He's a good kid, really. Hopefully, he won't give you too much trouble."

"Is that what Mom and Dad told you when they sent me to live with you?" Tony asked.

Eddie laughed. "They didn't tell me anything—just dropped you off and said, 'You look after him now,' and drove off."

Tony nodded, stomach clenching. He had a memory of standing in front of his brother's house, a suitcase and a couple of boxes at his feet, watching as his parents' sedan disappeared down the road. He had been sixteen but felt about twelve, wanting to cry but determined not to. Eddie hadn't said anything, simply picked up the suitcase and led the way into the house, to a room that obviously belonged to one of his two boys. "The kids can bunk together," Eddie had said, and dropped the suitcase beside the bed, with its *Star Wars* comforter. Tony had slept under that comforter for the next two years. Nothing in that house had felt like his. Nothing in his life had felt like his.

"I'll do my best for Chris," Tony said.

"Call me if you need anything," Eddie said. "And thanks. I owe you one."

They ended the call, and Tony tucked his phone away again. Eddie didn't owe him. Until today, Tony hadn't thought about what a debt he owed his brother. Despite their sometimes-difficult relationship, Eddie had saved him when he had nowhere else to turn. He would try to do the same for Chris.

Chapter Six

"Liz was only with us a couple of months, but she was one of those students who make an impression." Deborah Raymond, the English literature teacher who had first reported Liz missing, sat across the desk from Kelsey in her office at Eagle Mountain High School. A woman in her midforties with a long bob of dark blonde hair and stylish glasses, she had invited Kelsey to meet her at the school during her conference period Friday afternoon.

"What kind of impression?" Kelsey asked.

"A good one." Ms. Raymond smiled, revealing a slight gap between her upper front teeth. "You have to understand that I was in my first year of teaching then, so I wasn't that much older than my students. And Liz seemed more mature than most of her classmates—more of an adult than a teenager."

"You felt a connection to her?" Kelsey guessed.

"Yes and no." Ms. Raymond tilted her head, thoughtful. "Liz was friendly. She was popular with the other students. They were intrigued by this newcomer. Most of them had been together all through school, and Liz was an exotic outsider. She dressed a little more fashionably and had a navel piercing and this really independent attitude. She was charismatic and they were drawn to her. I was, too. But she didn't let anyone get too close. She never revealed a lot about her personal life or her inner feelings. A lot of kids that age wear all their emotions on the outside. I can tell by now when things aren't going well at home or a student has broken up with a boyfriend or had a fight with their best friend. Liz wasn't like that—I never really knew what she was thinking."

"What did you think when she didn't show up for class?" Kelsey asked.

"I thought she was probably ill. She was a good student, and she seemed to like school. She had never missed a class before—but, again, she had only been enrolled here a couple of months. One day out didn't concern me. On the second day, I asked some of her friends if any of them had heard from her, but they said they hadn't. I checked with the school office and learned this was an unexcused absence. No one had answered the phone when the attendance secretary called."

Fine lines creased her forehead, and she laced her fingers together. "By day three, I was concerned. I still thought Liz was probably ill, so I decided to go see her. I had the address on file with the school, so I drove over there."

Kelsey read real grief in Ms. Raymond's expression. "What did you find?" she prompted.

"The apartment was empty. Not just of people—of furniture and pictures and everything. The windows were dusty, and there were construction materials piled in the front room. It was clear no one had lived there in a long time."

"What did you think?"

"Honestly, my first emotion was hurt that Liz had lied to us all. Then I wondered why she would have done that. I became frightened and decided I had to contact the sheriff."

"Did Liz ever mention a boyfriend?"

"The investigators asked me that back then, too. But no, I never heard of Liz dating anyone, and she never spoke about a boyfriend—or any man in her life, really. Kids, especially the girls, talked to me about that kind of thing back then. I was close enough to their age that they felt comfortable confiding in me."

"Did Liz ever confide in you about anything else?"

"No. She was very good at keeping secrets without appearing to do so." She leaned forward. "I told her once I wanted to meet her parents. I knew all the other students' families. Most of them, I ran into regularly in town. But I hadn't met Liz's family yet. She smiled and said she was sure I would meet them soon, then changed the subject."

"Did that strike you as odd?" Kelsey asked.

"Not really. Not every teenager wants to talk about their parents. And not every kid has the ideal home life. But Liz never gave off any signs of being abused or neglected, so I didn't push."

"Did you have Tony Meisner in your class?" Kelsey wasn't sure why she asked the question, except she had been thinking a lot about Tony since their hike together. She was curious about him and what he had been like when he knew Liz.

Ms. Raymond smiled again. "Oh, yes. Tony was another of those students who has stayed with me," she said. "Of course, I still see him around town all the time."

"He was friends with Liz."

"He knew her," Ms. Raymond said. "In a class of only eighteen seniors, they all knew each other. But Tony and Liz weren't close. Tony was also a relative newcomer. He had moved to town the year before. He was quiet. Not unfriendly but definitely more of a loner. Liz was very outgoing."

"He found Liz's body," Kelsey said.

"Yes." Ms. Raymond picked up a pen and turned it over and over in her hand. "I think the experience shook him badly, as it would anyone," she said. "I remember the other students wanted to talk about it, and he wouldn't say anything. I worried about him. He seemed so alone. It was a relief when he came back to town and settled down and I could see he was doing well."

"He told me he had a crush on Liz," Kelsey said.

Ms. Raymond laughed. "I'm sure he did. All the boys in school did."

"But you never heard any gossip about Liz and a man outside of school, possibly someone older?"

Ms. Raymond shook her head. "I never did. I'm sorry. I wish I knew something that would help you, but I don't." She glanced at the clock. "And I'm afraid my conference period is almost over."

Kelsey pushed back her chair and stood. "Thank you for talking with me," she said. "It helps, knowing Liz had friends here."

"She did. We didn't know her very long, but we were all very upset to lose her."

As Kelsey drove away from the school, she thought about the language people used when talking about death. *Losing* Liz seemed as apt a description as any, as if they had misplaced her sister and might someday recover her. Nothing Kelsey or anyone else did would bring Liz back to life. But in coming to Eagle Mountain, Kelsey did feel she was finding her sister again.

TONY SPENT THE hours after work on Friday at Search and Rescue headquarters, inspecting and repacking gear. Hannah Richards had volunteered to help, and the two of them unloaded the specially equipped Jeep they used to transport volunteers and equipment, and laid out the climbing ropes, harnesses, packs, litters and assortment of safety and first aid supplies the group had used in Tuesday's rescue of a quartet of hikers cliffed out on a rocky ridge. The rescue had involved stringing out what felt like half their gear across that mountain face, and they had even hauled out their new drone to help locate the quartet ahead of the searchers' arrival.

Though everything had been assembled and made ready-to-go in case of another immediate callout, Tony wanted to take a closer look at all the gear while they had the time. There had been a lot of mud up there on the cliff, and it was easier to remove it after it had dried.

"How do you know Kelsey Chapman?" Hannah asked as she sponged mud off a climbing helmet.

Tony looked at her. "Why are you so nosy?" He had known Hannah most of her life, so he wasn't afraid to give her a hard time. He and her dad, Thad, had climbed together for years.

"I was just wondering how, if she's just visiting in town, you two hit it off so quickly."

He laid aside the climbing harness he had been examining and picked up another. "Her sister was a part of a rescue I was involved in years ago," he said. "Kelsey came to me and asked me to tell her the story."

Hannah's face clouded. "Was her sister a fatality?"

"Yes." He didn't elaborate. It wasn't his story to tell.

"I'm sorry," she said. "I guess I jumped to the wrong conclusion."

"What conclusion was that?"

Hannah blushed. "I thought the two of you were dating." She laughed. "But I guess that was silly."

"Why was it silly?"

"She's a lot younger than you, isn't she?" She flushed. "Not that younger women don't date older men, but you don't really…" She set aside the helmet. "I'm going to need some stronger cleaner for this. I think there's some in the closet."

Tony went back to counting carabiners but, in his mind, completed the sentence Hannah had been about to say. He didn't really date. Search and Rescue was full of single men and women in their prime, and members coupled, broke up and recoupled over the years. Some married. Some divorced. Some lived together long-term, and some had a new partner every month. But Tony never participated in that particular dance.

It wasn't that he had never dated. But he had never had a relationship with a woman that lasted more than a few weeks. He had never connected with others, always holding himself back.

His phone rang, and when he pulled it from his pocket, he was surprised to see an Iowa number. He only knew one person from Iowa, and his heart beat a little faster at the thought. "Hello?"

"Hi, Tony. It's Kelsey. I hope I'm not interrupting anything."

"No. I'm good. How are you?" *Why are you calling me?* he wanted to ask. But even he knew that sounded rude.

"I spent most of yesterday at the sheriff's department," she said. "They let me see their file on Liz. It was pretty grim."

He winced. "I'm sorry."

"It's okay. It was good that I saw it. And this morning, I talked to one of Liz's teachers, Deborah Raymond."

Tony remembered Ms. Raymond. Pretty and young, she had been a favorite with all of them. When Ms. Raymond spoke to him, he'd always had the impression she really cared.

"I have a lot more information about Liz's life here," Kelsey continued. "But I also have a lot more questions. I learned one good thing, though—the sheriff told me they have DNA evidence in storage, so if they ever find a suspect, they can test him. That makes me want to find Mountain Man even more."

"I found someone else for you to talk to," Tony said. "He was Search and Rescue captain when Liz was found. I don't think he can give you any information on Mountain Man, but maybe he can fill in some gaps about the scene that day."

"Oh, Tony, that is so wonderful. Thank you so much. So, what are you doing?"

"I'm at Search and Rescue headquarters, cleaning and packing gear. What are you doing?"

"I'm thinking about what I'm going to have for dinner."

"Yeah, I guess I'll be doing that soon, too."

"Want to have dinner with me?"

Was she asking him out? He opened his mouth to answer, but nothing came out.

"You don't have to if you're busy," she said. "I just didn't want to sit here by myself, all that stuff from Liz's case file in my head—"

"I'd love to have dinner with you," he blurted out. "Where?"

They settled on pizza at Mo's Pub at six thirty and ended the call.

Hannah returned as he was pocketing his phone. He began gathering up gear and returning it to the totes where it was stored. "Are we done already?" Hannah asked.

"I am," Tony said. "I need to go."

"What's the rush?"

He grinned. "I have a date."

It was worth saying the words just to see the surprise on her face.

TONY GOT TO Mo's ahead of Kelsey and snagged a booth at the back, where they would have more privacy. Even if all she wanted to do was talk about her sister, she would appreciate doing so without an audience. She slid into the booth across from him right at six thirty. She smelled fresh, like some kind of floral soap, and her hair was glossy. When she picked up the menu, he noticed her slender fingers and the half dozen silver rings she wore.

They made small talk, ordered pizza and beer; then she smiled across at him. "Let's talk about anything but murder," she said. "Tell me your best rescue story that has a happy ending."

"There are so many." He searched his memories for something to tell her. Something that wouldn't depress her. "If you do this work long enough, you learn how amazing people can be," he said. "Your fellow volunteers but also the people we rescue. You learn to never give up hope, because people can survive the most amazing things."

She leaned forward, rapt. "Such as?"

"We got a call one morning, a nice summer day. A family was hiking, and their ten-year-old daughter slipped and fell off the trail. A bad fall, at the base of a waterfall. When they described to the dispatcher where they were, we didn't see how the kid could survive. Ted Carruthers and I—he's the guy I said you need to talk to—packed a body bag, thinking we'd have to use it to bring her out. We ran up that mountain trail to get to her while the rest of the team followed. We ran for forty-five minutes. Ted was twenty years older than me and had a full pack, but I could barely keep up with him."

He stopped to sip his beer. "It must be harder, when it's kids who are injured," Kelsey said.

He nodded. "Her mom met us on the trail. It was a local family, so we all knew the names, even if we didn't know them personally. She said her husband had climbed down to the girl and covered her with all their jackets. This was a really high-up trail—almost ten thousand feet in elevation, and the girl had fallen three hundred feet or more. It was a real scramble getting down to her, but when we got there, she was still alive."

A server arrived to deliver their pizza, and Tony took a slice but didn't eat it right away. He was back at the base of that waterfall. "The falls were thundering, so we had to shout to hear each other. Within minutes, both of us and everything we had with us was wet. Snowmelt, so it was ice cold. The girl—her name was Susie—was really bad off. She had a closed head injury, a dislocated shoulder, a broken arm. She was having trouble breathing. Her dad was there, trying hard to keep it together, so we were trying to speak in a kind of code, not letting him know how bad off she was. On every scale we can use to measure medically, she was on the edge of dying."

He took a bite of pizza and chewed. He was surprised to see goose bumps on his forearm—visceral memory of how cold he had been that day.

"What happened next?" Kelsey asked after a pause.

He came back to the moment and the woman across from him. "The captain at the time, Mike Lawton, was trying to get a helicopter in to airlift the girl out of that canyon. They radioed they were at least an hour out, so we decided we needed to carry her down the trail to a flat area where the helicopter could meet us. By that time, the rest of the team had shown up. One of them brought a canister of oxygen, so we able to get a mask on her and try to help her breathe. It took us an hour and a half to get her down that steep, narrow trail to the helicopter, but she was still alive when we got there."

"And she lived?" Kelsey asked.

"She did." He cleared his throat, surprised he was so emotional about this after so long. "Three months later we had a picnic, and Susie and her family showed up. She was running around like a regular kid." She had thrown her arms around him in a hug, eyes shining, and he had had to turn away to keep from breaking down crying. "Her doctors said they had never seen anyone make such a quick recovery. They thought the fact that she had fallen in that cold water and become hypothermic so quickly—

plus her young age—had lessened the impact of her injuries."

"The fact that you all got to her so quickly must have made a difference, too," Kelsey said.

"I'm sure it did." He took another drink, feeling steadier. "Every time you go out on a call, you don't know what kind of impact you're going to have," he said. "I think that's why it never feels routine or boring."

"I think it's pretty amazing," she said.

She was smiling at him, her eyes full of such admiration that he began to feel self-conscious. "Enough about me," he said. "Tell me more about you. What kind of work do you do?"

"Nothing as exciting as search and rescue," she said. "I'm an accountant."

"In my day job, I'm a surveyor," he said. "That's not terribly exciting, either."

"But you get to be outside in this beautiful country."

"I get to be outside when it's raining and blowing snow, too," he said, and grinned.

"Go ahead and admit you love it," she teased.

And just like that, he was falling into an easy back-and-forth of conversation, laughing and maybe even flirting a little. Thirty-eight years old and he felt so far out of his depth, but gladly let her lead him along.

"Do you two need anything else?" Chris,

wearing a black apron and with his blond hair pulled back in a ponytail, grinned at them. "Hey, Uncle Tony. I told you I'd get a job." He readjusted the bus tub on one hip.

Tony was aware of Kelsey looking at him expectantly. "Kelsey, this is my nephew, Chris. Chris, this is Kelsey Chapman."

"Nice to meet you." Chris nodded. "Sorry for interrupting, but they sent me over to clear this table." He lowered his voice. "It's almost closing time."

Kelsey pushed her chair back from the table. "I guess we should go."

"No rush." Chris picked up their plates and slid them into the bus tub. "But you'll have to leave soon anyway."

Tony frowned and Chris hurried to collect the remaining dishes and left.

"He's cute," Kelsey said. "He looks a lot like you did at that age. At least, judging from the pictures I've seen."

"He just moved in with me." Tony looked into his empty beer mug. "I've lived alone for so long it's been a bit of an adjustment, but he's a good kid."

"I bet he really looks up to you," she said.

"Yeah, well, I've never been a role model before. I'm not sure how I feel about it."

She laughed as if he had made a joke, but he

liked the sound. It made him feel lighter somehow. He pulled out his wallet and reached for the check.

"No." She wrapped her fingers around his wrist. "This is my treat. I asked you out."

He started to argue, but she patted the back of his hand. "You can pay next time."

Next time. Next time they shared a meal. A date?

He pushed the thought aside. He had no idea how she felt about him. Maybe he was just a helpful older man she felt sorry for. He had always felt older than his real age, and she seemed so young and fresh. "You said you're ten years younger than Liz?" he asked as they exited the restaurant. "So, you're twenty-eight?"

"Yes. How old are you?"

"Thirty-eight."

She nodded but made no further comment as they walked back to the Alpiner Inn. The night was clear and not too cold, the stars sharp as broken glass overhead. Kelsey looked up at them. "This really is the most beautiful place," she said.

"Yes," he agreed, but he wasn't looking at the sky. He was taking advantage of her distraction to look at her—the elegant arc of her neck as she tilted her head back, the silken fall of her hair down her back.

They stopped outside the inn, and she took both his hands in hers. “Thank you for saving me from a depressing evening in my room,” she said. “I’m feeling much better now.”

“Thank *you*,” he said. “It’s not often I have such good company.” Did that sound too stilted? He never knew what to say.

“I’ll see you soon,” she said. She leaned forward and pressed her lips to his cheek, then released his hands and hurried inside, leaving him dazed and half believing he had dreamed the whole evening.

Chapter Seven

"Hi, Mom, how are you doing today?" Kelsey sat on the edge of the bed Saturday morning, picturing her mom in the living room of the home Kelsey had grown up in. She could hear the television playing in the background—some morning-news program, she guessed.

"I'm as well as can be expected," her mother said—her usual answer. "Thank you for the newspaper article about Liz. It was hard to read, but I appreciated the picture. It was one of my favorites of her."

Kelsey again felt a flash of anger at her father, who, in refusing to keep any reminders of Liz, had deprived the rest of them of so many precious memories. "Is the young man in the photo the one you talked to?" her mother asked.

"He is, but he's not so young now. He's thirty-eight."

"Liz would be thirty-eight." *Does everyone who has lost a loved one do this?* Kelsey wondered. *Automatically calculate the age the person would be right now if they had lived?*

"But he remembers Liz," her mother added.

"He remembers her. He's been very helpful." Tony had made some of the hardest parts of this journey not so hard. He was so quiet and calm. So capable. He looked like a college professor, until you noticed the corded muscles in his arms and felt his rock-hard biceps. Someone first meeting him might mistake him for meek until they learned he routinely did incredible things like run up mountain trails, descend cliffs on a rope or wade in ice-cold water in order to save the lives of strangers. No city gym rat could compete with that when it came to sexiness.

The thought jolted her a little, but the surprise quickly faded. Why shouldn't she think Tony was sexy? He was different from the men she usually dated—older, less polished. But different was good.

Besides, they weren't dating. He was her friend. Someone who was guiding her through a difficult time.

She realized her mother was talking to her. "I'm sorry, Mom, what did you say?"

"Have you found out anything else about Liz?"

"I spoke with the teacher who reported Liz missing. She said Liz was very popular."

"Of course she was," Mary said. "She was beautiful and bright. Everyone who knew her loved her."

Kelsey had always thought of her sister that way, but had Liz really been so perfect? Was her sister dead because of random circumstances or because of her own bad choices? "The teacher said Liz was popular but that she also didn't tell people details about her life. Everyone here thought she was living with her family."

"She would have been here with us if not for that man," Mary said. "Did the teacher say anything about him?"

Kelsey knew her mother meant Mountain Man. "She said Liz kept him a secret. No one here seems to have known about him. The sheriff's deputies interviewed everyone who knew Liz, and none of them had heard of any man in her life."

"He was a real person. You need to find him."

They both let that thought sink in, along with the question that hung over this whole expedition to Eagle Mountain: How do you find a man who had remained invisible for twenty years?

"What are you doing today?" her mother asked.

"I'm going to the library to look at the high school yearbook from when Liz was here," Kelsey said. "I'm hoping to make a list of names of classmates who knew her and find as many of them as possible to talk to while I'm here." Surely Liz would have told at least one girlfriend about the older man she was living with. At home in Iowa, Liz had annoyed them all, talking about Mountain Man incessantly, though she never used his name. Why had her parents not seen his insistence on anonymity as a warning sign? She couldn't ask her mother. Why contribute more to her guilt and pain?

"I'll let you go, then," her mother said, and ended the call.

That was Mom—not sentimental or concerned about manners. She had tried to get closer to Kelsey after her husband died, but Kelsey thought she was out of practice. Liz was the only thing they had real conversations about. If Kelsey tried to talk about her job or her apartment or a movie she had seen, Mom lost interest. Kelsey wanted to be there for her, to be a real daughter. But it was hard when her mother didn't feel like a real mother. Not the person concerned with the details of her life that her friends' mothers were. They complained of feeling stifled by love sometimes, but Kelsey wanted to tell them being stifled was better than being starved.

SATURDAY AFTERNOON, Tony scanned the listing of Search and Rescue donors until he found the name he wanted. Then he punched in the number for Jessica Stringfellow, now Jessica Macintosh. "Hello, Jessica? It's Tony Meisner."

"Hey, Tony," she said as if it had not been at least fifteen years since they had more than nodded on the street.

"This is going to seem out of the blue, but do you remember that girl who went to school with us who went missing? Liz Chapman?"

"Oh my goodness. Of course I remember Liz. That was terrible what happened to her. You're the one who found her body, weren't you?"

"I did. Her sister is in town, and she asked me if I knew any of Liz's friends who might talk to her, and I thought of you."

"She wants to talk to me about Liz? I don't know what I can tell her."

"She's just trying to come to terms with what happened, I think. She was a little kid when Liz left home, and she wants to hear what Liz was like, that kind of thing."

"Well, sure, I can talk to her."

"Do you know anyone else I can ask? People who knew Liz and might have been close to her?"

"There were lots of us who knew her, but she was kind of an odd duck, you know? Lots of fun to be around and really nice, but she didn't let people get too close. It was like she had secrets she was keeping. And I guess it turned out she was. I mean, we were all shocked when we found out she had moved here on her own, without her parents, and that she may have been involved with some mysterious older man. It was like something out of a movie."

"Who else can I call who would talk to her?" he asked again.

"Let me call," Jessica said. "I can think of a few people who are still around. I'll get back to you about when we can meet. It's really sweet of you to help the sister."

He couldn't remember anyone ever calling him *sweet*. "I couldn't turn down someone who asked for help," he said.

"Some people would, you know."

He ended the call, and after only a moment's hesitation, he called Kelsey.

"Hello?"

"Is everything okay?" he asked. "You sound out of breath."

"I'm just walking around the park. Trying to get some exercise, but the altitude has me puffing a little."

"If you stick around long enough, you'll get used to it." Why had he said that? When she had all the answers she could find here, she would leave and go back to Iowa. Back to accounting and her mom and whatever man she was seeing—though she hadn't mentioned a relationship, had she?

"I spent this morning at the library, looking at her class yearbook," she said. "I found some good pictures of her. Apparently, she really dove right into high school life—volleyball team, yearbook committee, Spanish club."

"It's like that in a small school," he said. "There were only eighteen students in our graduating class."

"That must have made relationships awkward. And prom."

He laughed. "Relationships *are* awkward. Especially when you're a teen. But a lot of kids dated kids from nearby towns, and we had a joint prom with Delta."

"There was a photo of you in there, too, in your search and rescue gear. Hubba, hubba."

He laughed again. "I doubt many girls were swooning over the SAR geek."

"Oh, I think you're wrong there. You had that shy-guy demeanor that some women find very sexy. And there's the whole *risking your life for others* mystique. I bet you Search and Rescue guys even have groupies."

He had heard stories—though if any women had ever hit on him after a rescue, he had been oblivious. "If any of the high school girls were admiring me from afar, I was too awkward to notice," he said.

"You were too busy crushing on my sister."

"Who didn't know I was alive."

"Liz took it for granted that men admired her," Kelsey said. "I don't think she was arrogant about it—she just knew she was beautiful."

"You look a lot like her, you know."

"People have told me that, but I don't see it. I mean, we have the same hair, but I think part of beauty is attitude. Liz had it but I don't."

"There are all kinds of attitude and all kinds of beauty," he said, then winced, sure he sounded impossibly cringeworthy. Time to change the subject. "I talked to one of Liz's friends. She's going to contact some others and arrange a meeting so you can talk to them all."

"And the former SAR commander you mentioned, too. How can I get in touch with him?"

"I'll run him to ground," Tony said. "Maybe the three of us can get together for a drink later today."

"That would be great. And remember—this time, you're paying." She was still laughing when she ended the call. She didn't laugh like Liz. Kelsey's mirth was warmer and softer, a little more restrained. As if she wasn't ready to give everything away just yet.

Chris shuffled into the room, shirtless and

toweling his hair, the smell of herbal shampoo heralding his arrival. "Was that Kelsey on the phone?" he asked.

"Nosy," Tony said.

"Hey, don't get all up in my face about it. I liked her." He gave Tony a thumbs-up. "You're doing all right for yourself, with the hot younger girlfriend and all."

"Kelsey isn't my girlfriend."

"But you want her to be." Chris laughed. "Don't lie. You should have seen the expression on your face while you were talking to her."

Tony glared, but that only made Chris laugh more. "For what it's worth, I think she was pretty into you, too," Chris said.

"Since when are you an expert?"

"I've been doing mostly restaurant work for a few years now. A good server has to be able to read body language, know when someone is in a good mood or upset about something. The secret to good tips is knowing how to read people."

"You're not a server," Tony said. "You're a busboy."

"I'm a busboy now, but I'm going to get promoted. It's just a matter of time."

"Is that what you want to do for the rest of your life? Wait tables?"

Chris shrugged. "Probably not, but it's good for now."

"But what about the future?" Tony asked.

"What about it?" He tossed the towel back toward the bathroom and missed. It landed in a wet heap on the hall floor. "Nice talking to you, but I have to get going."

Tony stared after him, a feeling he couldn't identify surging through him. With a start, he realized the emotion was jealousy. Did he envy Chris more for his youth or his confidence? A little of both, probably.

Had Chris been right—that Kelsey was into Tony? If his own attraction to her was so obvious to his nephew, he needed to be more careful not to let other people see it. Having all your teenage friends know that you were crushing on the girl they all wanted, too, was very different from a grown man infatuated with a newcomer who was ten years younger. He didn't want anyone—especially Kelsey—to get the wrong idea.

TED CARRUTHERS LOOKED pretty much as Kelsey had pictured him when Tony had described Ted as "an old cowboy and search and rescue veteran." When she walked into Mo's at seven that evening, she spotted the silver-haired man in the Western shirt and boots in the booth before she even saw Tony across from him. He had the leathered skin of men in Charlie Russell paintings, a drooping mustache and tinted aviator glasses.

Tony stood as Kelsey approached the table, and Ted shoved to his feet as well. "Kelsey, this is Ted Carruthers. Ted, Kelsey Chapman."

Ted shook her hand. "It's nice to meet you," he said. "Though I don't know how much help I can be to you. I didn't know your sister."

Kelsey slid into the booth across from Ted, who had a large glass of beer in front of him. Beside her, Tony sipped from a glass of what looked like iced tea. "Just tell me about the day Search and Rescue retrieved her body," she said.

"Tony here made the call, you know." Ted nodded at his friend. "He was just a kid, and I don't know if he'd ever seen a dead body before."

"I hadn't," Tony said.

Ted grimaced. "It's worse when it's someone you know. Of course, that happens a lot when you work search and rescue in a small remote town. Eventually, you know a lot of the people you help. And some who die."

"What was the weather like that day?" Kelsey asked.

Ted frowned. "The weather? What difference does the weather make?"

"I'm trying to picture in my mind what it was like."

Ted shook his head. "Suit yourself." He tilted his head back. "Let's see. It was sunny. A little breeze. Good conditions for a rescue, and right near a pretty easy trail. The biggest hassle was waiting around until the sheriff's deputies finished collecting all their evidence." He smirked. "Not that it took that long. There were only three deputies back then, and the sheriff. He and one of the deputies showed up at the scene initially. Then he called in the third. They crawled around in the grass and rocks for the better part of an hour and came up with a gum wrapper and some other trash that could have been left by who knows who. I wouldn't call it *evidence*."

"Was anyone else there who shouldn't have been?" Kelsey asked. "Any hikers or tourists or anything?"

Ted took a long swallow of beer before he answered. "Nobody else," he said. "We didn't have the crowds of tourists in town back then that we do now." He rubbed his chin. "Tony was there, of course. And Mel Wheeler. Do you remember him?" he asked Tony.

"Mel lives in Phoenix now," Tony said.

"That's right. Let's see. Peggy Pendleton was there, and that fellow from—where was it, Mexico?"

"Peru. Alejandro Garcia."

"Right. That was it." He shrugged. "We didn't need many people for that kind of mission. It was just a matter of loading everything on the litter and carrying it down."

Kelsey kept her face expressionless, refusing to let him see her react to his reference to Liz as "everything." "Tell me about the other volunteers," she said. "What was Alejandro like?" The name sounded sexy.

"He was a professional climber out of South America," Ted said. "He worked as a local guide for a couple of years, and he could climb anything." He chuckled. "I was around forty then and in the best shape of my life. But Alejandro, at fifty-two, could climb rings around any of us." He jerked his head in Tony's direction once more. "He was even better than this kid."

"Alejandro was married and had five children," Tony said.

So, unlikely to have either appealed to Liz or to be able to hide her existence from his wife and many children. "What about Mel Wheeler?"

"Thirtysomething carpenter from Paradise," Ted said.

"He was only with us for the one year," Tony said.

"And he's in Phoenix now?" she asked.

"Last I heard," Tony said.

Kelsey made a mental note to check into Mel

Wheeler. Maybe he was Mountain Man and had left town to avoid detection after Liz had died.

Ted drained the last of his beer and set the empty glass down with a thunk. "Anything else you want to know?"

She had intended to ask him the same questions she had asked Tony: What had Liz looked like when they found her? Had he noticed anything unusual? But he didn't have Tony's sensitivity or the attention to detail she had found in the sheriff's deputy's reports. There was no sense asking him to repeat what she had already gleaned elsewhere. "Did you know Liz?" she asked. "Before she died?"

He shook his head. "No reason I would. Like I said, I was forty. She was a kid."

A kid who never got to grow up, Kelsey thought. "Thank you for talking with me," she said.

"I don't see how I've helped." He stood. "Thanks for the beer," he said to Tony, and left.

"TED CAN BE a crotchety old guy," Tony said when Ted was gone.

"He's given me a couple of names to look into," she said. "Alejandro and Mel."

"I don't think either of them killed Liz," Tony said. "I could be wrong, but I was there that day and they didn't show a flicker of recognition."

"Maybe a sociopath wouldn't."

"I don't think all killers are sociopaths."

"I'm no expert, but I think a man who would lure a young woman away from her family only to kill her a few weeks later has something wired wrong in them."

"You're right. And I guess that kind of thing doesn't always show on the outside."

She turned to look at him. The booth was small, forcing them to sit close together, their thighs almost touching. "Thanks for listening to me and for trying to help. You must have a lot of other things you could be doing with your time."

"Not really. And you've made me curious now. I want to see how all this works out."

"Have you heard any more from Liz's friends?"

He nodded. "Jessica MacIntosh—she used to be Jessica Stringfellow—has invited a few of Liz's classmates to her house tomorrow night. She says you can come and meet them, and they'll tell you what they know."

"And you waited to tell me this?" She swatted his arm—more of a brush of her fingers against his bicep.

"I knew Ted wouldn't be an easy interview, so I saved the good news for last."

"He wasn't that bad."

"He can be a little insensitive."

"Not everyone is as thoughtful as you."

She was looking at him again, eyes lingering in a way that made him feel as if she was trying to peel back the layers. He faced forward once more. "Do you want to order dinner?"

"Do you?"

"Could you stand to eat with me two nights in a row?"

"I think I could manage." She reached past him and plucked a menu from behind the salt and pepper shakers. The side of her breast brushed his shoulder, and sensation shuddered through him. "Besides," she said, "you owe me a meal."

"Then I had better pay up," he said, keeping his tone light. Inside, he was thinking he was too old to be this foolish. Thirty-eight-year-old men didn't have crushes on women who were out of their reach.

Chapter Eight

Jessica and Andrew MacIntosh lived in a cedar-sided cabin in a heavily treed neighborhood up Carolina Gulch, on the south side of Eagle Mountain. As Tony guided his Toyota up the dozen switchbacks leading to the MacIntosh home Saturday evening, Kelsey gaped out the window at the spectacular vistas and sheer drop-offs, icy waterfalls, snow-capped peaks and evergreen-choked drainages. It was the kind of scenery that either frightened people into never coming back or made them return again and again, leading many to up and move from wherever they had called home before.

"What do people do for a living around here?" she asked.

"A lot of them work online," he said. "Andy MacIntosh is a pilot, and Jessica builds websites, I think. I'm not a techie, so I'm not exactly sure."

The driveway was full of cars by the time

they arrived, so Tony parked on the street, and he and Kelsey walked up to the house. The home had plenty of windows to take advantage of the view and decks on three sides for relaxing outdoors. Jessica, barefoot and in wide-legged black pants and a multicolored tunic, greeted them at the door. She wore her hair shorter than in high school, and she wasn't as slender, but she had the same smile that had stood out in every photo of the Eagle Mountain cheer squad. "Come in, come in." She ushered them inside. "Tony, it's so good to see you. I see your picture in the paper all the time, on those amazing rescues."

"Jessica, this is Kelsey Chapman," he said.

"It's nice to meet you, Kelsey," Jessica said. "You can hang your coats in that closet. Then come on through to the living room, and I'll introduce you to everyone else."

Tony was surprised to find six people besides Jessica and her husband seated on sofas and chairs in the expansive great room of the MacIntosh home. Jessica introduced Marcus White, who had sat on the bench at basketball games with Tony; Madison Gruenwald, who had been a plump, vivacious redhead and now was a thin, still-vivacious woman with dyed purple hair. Veronica Olivares was another volleyball player, whose dark hair had been cut short but was otherwise looking remarkably as she had in their senior year. Taylor Redmond, Sarah Fish and Darla Cash rounded out the six. Taylor and Sarah had also played volleyball, while Darla had worked with Liz on the yearbook committee.

"Let me get you a glass of wine," Jessica said. "And help yourself to snacks." She indicated the platters of hors d'oeuvres set out on the large coffee table in the center of the seating area.

While Jessica went around the room with wine bottles, everyone made small talk with Kelsey. Where did she live? What kind of work did she do? How did she know Tony?

Half-involved in a conversation with Marcus, Tony strained his ears to hear Kelsey's answer to the last question. "Tony was with the Search and Rescue team that retrieved Liz's body," she said. "He's been helping me find out as much as I can about what happened to her."

"That was so terrible," Veronica said. "We were all just in shock when we found out."

"They never found whoever did it, did they?" Andy asked. He was a few years older than the rest of them and from Houston, but Jessica must have told him Liz's story.

"They never did," Marcus said. "I think they decided it was some kind of random killer, you know? Like Ted Bundy."

"What questions did you have for us?" Jessica asked, bringing the conversation back to the point of the get-together.

"What did you know about Liz?" Kelsey asked. "What did she tell you about herself—her history?"

The other people in the room exchanged looks as if waiting for someone else to go first. "Liz didn't really talk about herself much," Madison finally said. "I think I knew she had moved here from Iowa or Ohio or somewhere in the Midwest."

The others nodded in agreement. "She was pretty and popular, and we didn't really care where she was from," Marcus said.

"What did she say about her family or her living situation?" Kelsey asked.

"We never talked about that stuff," Madison said.

"I asked her once why she never talked about her mom and dad," Veronica said. "She said they were good people—they just didn't understand her. Which was all of our parents, right?" She rolled her eyes. "My kids are only seven and nine, and already I'm dreading those teenage years. No matter what I do as a mom, it won't be right. That's just how it is."

More agreement and some chuckles from the others. "What about guys?" Kelsey asked. "Did she go out with anyone at school? Or with anyone else? Did you ever see her with a guy or hear her talk about a boyfriend?"

"No boyfriend," Darla said. "I asked her once, and she said relationships were too complicated and she just wanted to have fun. Which I thought was wild because she had all these boys who were wild about her, and it was all I could do to get Bobby Preston to ask me to prom."

More laughter. "There was always Ben Everett," someone—Tony didn't see who—said.

"Yes, Ben!" Taylor said. "I know he asked her to the prom that year, though I don't know if she accepted or not."

"He asked her out more than that," Marcus said. "Maybe four or five times. He really had it bad for her." He cast a sideways glance at Tony. "We all crushed on her a little. I mean, she was the new girl, and so pretty and friendly and everything. But Ben had it really bad."

"What about that one night at the ice-cream parlor?" Madison asked. "You remember? A bunch of us were there, and Liz said she was meeting someone. But she wouldn't say who it was."

"Oh my gosh, I forgot all about that!" Jessica said. "But I remember. Liz was all mysterious, and I got the impression she wanted us to think this guy was an older guy—a real man and not just some boy from school."

"She said that? That he was older?" Kelsey asked.

"She didn't really say it," Taylor said. "But we were all trying to find out who it was, and she said something like, 'Oh, it's not a *boy* from school.' Like that, with the emphasis on *boy*."

"I don't think it was Ben," Sarah said. "Because I dated him for a while after Liz died, and if he had ever gone out with her, I'm sure he would have said something. Before him, I didn't know boys could talk so much."

The other women laughed. The men looked uncomfortable. "Did anyone see this guy?" Kelsey asked. "The one she was meeting that night at the ice-cream parlor?"

Everyone shook their heads. "I told Madison I was going to follow Liz and get a look at the guy," Jessica said. "But I had to go to the bathroom, and when I came out, Liz was already gone. Then someone asked me about a play I had made in the last game we had had against Delta, and I forgot all about Liz's mystery man."

"Did you tell the sheriff's department about this guy?" Kelsey asked.

Jessica frowned. "There wasn't really anything to tell, was there? She could even have been making the whole thing up. I mean, there was so much she didn't tell us. Maybe she wanted us all to believe she was dating some glamorous older man, when really she was just walking home alone."

"So, no one saw Liz with any man?" she asked.

Veronica looked thoughtful. "You know, I came in right before Liz left. Ted Carruthers was standing a few doors down from the ice-cream parlor, smoking a cigarette. You might ask him if he saw anything."

Kelsey glanced at Tony. "We talked to Ted yesterday, but I'll ask him about that night." She glanced at the notes she had been making. "Do you have any idea how I can get in touch with Ben?"

Again, they exchanged glances. "I don't think I've seen or heard from him since graduation," Jessica said.

"Didn't he go out of state for college?" Sarah asked. "Tennessee or Michigan or something?"

"I know the sheriff questioned him at the time," Veronica said.

"Oh, he talked about that," Madison said. "He said two big officers backed him into a corner and accused him of strangling Liz. They said he did it because she wouldn't go out with him. He said he was terrified, and I believe it. He was shaking when he told me."

"I think I heard they took his DNA and it didn't match up with the evidence they found," Marcus said.

"I'd still like to talk to him," Kelsey said. "If he was always watching Liz, maybe he saw her with another man some time."

"All of us talked to the police after Liz went missing," Madison said. "And again after they found her body. We thought we knew her—that she was our friend. But then we found out there was so much we didn't know."

"We thought she was like us," Taylor said. "A kid living with her parents. Not a girl with this secret life none of us knew about."

"Is there anyone else the police interviewed?" Kelsey asked.

Jessica laughed. "Well, there was Tony."

All eyes focused on him. "That's right!" Madison said. "For a while there, Tony was the number one suspect." She leaned toward him. "I guess because you found the body but also because you were always mooning after her."

"Don't blush," Jessica said as his face heated. "All the guys in school had a crush on Liz. And all the girls were jealous of her, but none of us killed her."

The conversation shifted then to more-general high school reminiscences. As they fell into recollections of games and dances and pranks,

Tony felt more and more distanced. Kelsey touched his elbow and leaned over to whisper, "I think we can go now."

They thanked Jessica and said goodbye to everyone else. Tony didn't say anything else until they were halfway down the long series of switchbacks. The air between them was as brittle as a skim of ice. "I didn't kill your sister," he said finally. "I didn't have anything to do with her death."

She shifted toward him, her features barely discernible in the darkness. "Did the sheriff really suspect you?" she asked.

"The sheriff talked to me. One of his deputies accused me of killing her, then waiting to find the body so I could be a hero." He gripped the steering wheel more tightly, remembering the hot, claustrophobic room where they had questioned him; the smell of his own fear-sweat, metallic in the air. "They tested my DNA and cleared me."

She nodded. "I wasn't going to ask."

"I wanted you to know."

"I never thought you killed her." The leather of the car seat creaked as she shifted position again. "What about Ben Everett? Did you know him?"

"As well as I knew anyone. He was smart. Class salutatorian. His dad was a doctor in the

ER in Junction, and he had three or four older sisters. He was the only one who had the nerve to ask Liz out, but I don't think he would kill her. And anyway, they tested his DNA, too."

She sighed, a weary sound. "I'd still like to talk to him. And I'll talk to Ted again, too. What do you think he was doing there that night?"

Tony thought back to the location of the ice-cream parlor. There was a T-shirt shop there now. "There was a bar two doors down from there," he said. "The White Elephant Tavern. It was a place where cowboys hung out. Ted was probably there and had stepped out for a smoke."

She nodded. "I need to talk to him again."

"There's a meeting at SAR headquarters tomorrow morning," Tony said. "You could talk to Ted then."

"I thought he was retired from search and rescue work?"

"He doesn't go on calls anymore, but he still comes to meetings. And he's our historian."

"What does a SAR historian do?"

"He writes up a narrative about each call—who was there, what the call involved, the outcome. It's a good record of all the calls over the years."

"Is there a write-up about Liz's call?"

"We'll ask him. I don't know who was keeping records back then, but Ted will know."

"Maybe he saw this man Liz was supposedly meeting that night at the ice-cream parlor."

"If there *was* a man," Tony said.

"There had to be someone," Kelsey said. "We don't know much, but we know for sure Liz didn't kill herself."

Chapter Nine

Kelsey slept poorly that night, her sleep interrupted by snatches of the conversation with Liz's friends. They had painted a picture of the same Liz whom Kelsey had known—pretty, popular and outgoing, with a large circle of friends. Yet there had been a shadow side of her, living a second life she let no one else see. The mood in the room hadn't been unfriendly, but there had been an underlying current of—not animosity but distrust. They felt betrayed by the things Liz hadn't told them.

Kelsey felt that betrayal, too. Why had Liz kept so many secrets? Why had she lied about so much, from the real name of the man she was seeing to her address on school records? Kelsey didn't even understand how her sister had managed to enroll in school, but maybe because she was eighteen, she had enrolled herself and the authorities believed what she had told them.

Was she secretive because Mountain Man had

told her to be—forced her to be? Or had she been indulging her sense of drama, enjoying being a woman of mystery, with a secret affair no one knew about?

Someone must know something. Eagle Mountain was a small town. People paid attention, especially to a pretty, new girl. How was it that no one knew anything to help identify Liz's Mountain Man?

She recalled the stricken look on Tony's face when Madison had mentioned that he had been a suspect in Liz's murder. She never would have believed he would kill anyone, but she was grateful for the DNA test to remove all doubt. She would have hated to have that between them, even if only in the form of him worrying about her doubting him.

Odd that she had met him such a short time ago yet felt she knew him so well. She had imagined having to do all her investigating of Liz's death on her own. Instead, she had him to bounce ideas off of and help arrange meetings with people who might help her, like Liz's friends, and Ted Carruthers. She had never expected to be so lucky.

The next morning, she tried to cover the dark shadows beneath her eyes with makeup and drove up the steep county road to Search and Rescue headquarters. The lot was full of cars, and she wondered if an emergency had summoned all the volunteers. As she was walking up to the building, Hannah Richards hailed her. "Hey, Kelsey."

Hannah was with a handsome brown-haired man she introduced as her fiancé, Jake Gwynne. "Are you thinking of joining Eagle Mountain Search and Rescue?" Hannah asked.

"No, I just needed to talk to Ted Carruthers for a minute," Kelsey said. "I understand he was the captain of Search and Rescue when Liz's body was found. I'll leave before the meeting."

"I'm sure Ted is around here somewhere," Hannah said.

More than a dozen people milled about inside the cavernous space of the building's main room. Kelsey looked around for Tony but spotted Ted first. He looked surprised to see her. "Couldn't get enough of us, could you?" he asked.

"I had a couple more questions for you." She looked around the crowded room. "Can we go somewhere to talk for a minute?"

He frowned and she thought he was going to say no. Instead, he jerked his head toward the back of the room. "This way."

She followed him through a plain metal door to a narrow dirt lot behind the building. Wind whipped around the corner, sending snow spiraling about their knees. Ted leaned against the metal siding of the building, arms folded over his chest. Though his face showed the weathered lines of a man in his sixties, the muscles of his arms bulged with the strength of a younger man. “What do you want to know?” he asked.

“I talked to some of Liz’s friends last night,” she said. “I’m trying to find out about the man Liz was supposedly dating. She called him Mountain Man whenever she mentioned him to my mom and dad. No one seems to have heard of him or to have ever seen her with anyone in particular.”

“How am I supposed to know anything about that?” he asked.

“Her friends remembered one night when they were gathered at an ice-cream parlor in town. Liz told them she was meeting someone, an older man she was dating—or at least, not a high school boy. None of them saw the guy when Liz went out to meet him, but one of them remembered seeing you on the sidewalk near the ice-cream parlor, smoking a cigarette. I wondered if you saw the guy—maybe when Liz came out to meet him?”

Ted stared at her, annoyance twisting his mouth. “You expect me to remember something that happened one random night over twenty years ago, to a girl I didn’t even know?”

"Think about it," she said. "Maybe you remember."

He shook his head. "I'm sorry you lost your sister, but this is ridiculous. I was forty years old back then. I had my own busy life. I wouldn't have paid much attention to a bunch of kids."

Kelsey fought disappointment. "It may seem foolish to you, but you might have remembered," she said. "I had to take the chance and ask. I'm sorry I bothered you."

She turned to leave, but his hand on her shoulder stopped her. "Hey," he said.

She turned to look at him, and he dropped his hand. "I'm sorry I went off on you," he said. "I'm just a grouchy old guy. I wish I could help you, but I just can't."

She nodded. "Thanks."

"Look," he said. "You didn't ask my advice, but I'm going to give it to you anyway because I'm a lot older than you, and you don't get old without learning a few things." He went on, not waiting for her to reply. "I know you came here with some idea that you were going to bring this all out in the open and find out what really happened to your sister, but think what you're asking. It's been over twenty years, and in all that time, no one has found one shred of evidence to point to your sister's killer. If there was anything out there, they would have found it by now. If someone knew something, they would have spoken up. This is a small town. There are no secrets here. How are you—someone who isn't a trained investigator or even a law enforcement officer—going to find what other people haven't found before you?"

"I don't have to solve the crime," she said. "All I have to do is find a credible suspect. Someone whose DNA can be compared to the evidence on file at the sheriff's department."

"What kind of evidence?" Ted asked.

"Skin cells under Liz's fingernails, where she fought with her killer. If I find anyone who might be the man who lured her to Eagle Mountain, he can be tested. If he's a match, then they'll have Liz's killer."

"And if they don't?"

"Then I'll have to keep looking." She pushed open the door and went back inside. Saying those words out loud made the task ahead of her almost overwhelming, despite her bravado. The truth was, while reading the files and talking to people made Kelsey feel closer to Liz, she had discovered nothing to help her find out who had ended her sister's life.

THOUGH MANY OF the calls Search and Rescue responded to involved vacationers or travelers on the mountain highway, it wasn't unusual for volunteers to know the people they were called to assist. But Tony didn't recognize the description of the Jeep that had rolled at what was locally known as Dead Man's Curve on the drive down from Dixon Pass. "Driver and passenger both responsive but trapped in the vehicle," Sheri said when the team assembled on Sunday afternoon on the roadside above where the Jeep had gone over. "Eldon and Jake, you go down to the vehicle," she directed. "Caleb and Danny, you go with them. Tony, you help with the ropes up here."

Tony nodded. This time last year, he would have been the one leading the climb down, but since his accident, he'd been relegated to helping with the gear. He told himself that was okay. He was here to contribute in whatever way he could. But a small part of him acknowledged wanting to be climbing down that rope, more directly involved in the rescue instead of waiting for someone to need him up here.

Within twenty minutes, Eldon and the others had reached the vehicle, stabilized it and deployed the Jaws of Life to free the two occupants. Tony's shoulder-mounted radio crackled; Danny's voice came over the speaker. "Hey, Tony. The passenger says he's related to you. Some kid named Chris."

Tony's chest constricted, and he almost

dropped the brake-bar rack he was holding. "Chris Meisner is my nephew," he said. "Is he okay?"

"He's going to be sore for a while, but so far it doesn't look like anything serious," Danny said. "I didn't think you had any family in town."

"He hasn't been here long," Tony said. "You're sure he's okay?"

"He's good, but you can check him out yourself. We're going to send him up in a few minutes."

Apparently, Chris had been deemed fit enough to make the climb out of the canyon under his own power, assisted by Caleb. Tony waited as the two of them climbed up over the rim, then hurried to help his nephew out of the harness and helmet. "What happened?" he asked, one hand on Chris's arm.

"Blake and I were talking, and the next thing I know, we're sailing out into nothing." Chris grinned, but his face was paper white beneath his tan, and his laughter sounded forced. "I guess we missed the curve."

"Come over here and sit down." Tony led him to the Search and Rescue vehicle, known as the Beast, and sat him on the back bumper. "Who is Blake?"

"A guy I work with at Mo's."

Tony handed the young man a bottle of water.

"Thanks." But Chris's hands shook so badly Tony had to open the water for him. "That was wild," Chris said, then chugged the water.

"You're sure you're okay?" Tony bent to look in Chris's eyes. "Did you hit your head? How does your back feel?"

"I don't think I hit my head." He ran a hand through his hair. "No bumps or blood. I banged my knee on the dash." He rubbed his left kneecap, then massaged the back of his neck. "Danny said I might have a neck strain, but honestly, I'm okay." He looked around. "How's Blake?"

Tony looked over his shoulder to where others were hauling the litter with the Jeep's driver on board. He should really be over there helping, but he couldn't bring himself to leave Chris. "I'll check on him in a bit," he said. "Was he conscious when you left him?"

Chris laughed again, sounding more relaxed this time. "He was swearing a blue streak and pounding on the steering wheel, furious that he'd torn up his Jeep. He's only had it a few months." His expression sobered. "I think Danny said something about a broken bone? And he had some cuts from the windshield glass." He stared out toward the canyon. "It's wild, isn't it? I can't believe we both walked away from something like that. Well, Blake isn't *walking*, but he will be soon."

Tony clapped him on the back, his throat tight. "I'm glad you're okay," he managed to say. "I'm going to go check on your friend."

Blake was sitting up, being examined by one of the paramedics. Tony pulled Danny aside. "Is he going to be okay?"

"Probable fracture of the distal radius, though he'll need x-rays to confirm," Danny said. "And he's got one cut that might need a few stitches." He looked back toward Chris. "Your nephew got off with hardly a scratch. So, how long has he been in town?"

"He moved in three days ago."

"I never heard you mention it," Danny said.

"It didn't come up." Tony didn't talk about his personal life much. Before, when he'd lived alone, there wasn't much to say. Chris moving in hadn't really changed that.

"Go be with him," Danny said. "The rest of us can clean up here."

Tony started to argue but thought better of it and returned to Chris, who stood at his approach. Chris drained the rest of the water and crushed the plastic bottle. "So, this is what you do, huh?" He looked around at the ambulance crew and the volunteers gathering up supplies. "Go out and rescue hapless strangers?"

"Some of them not so hapless. And some of them not strangers. Yeah."

Chris nodded. "Cool." He looked toward the drop-off, then away. "I don't think I could do that. I mean, the climbing and stuff would be cool, but dealing with bleeding people..." He shook his head. "I think I'm too empathetic, you know?"

And I'm not empathetic enough, Tony thought. But it wasn't that he didn't care about people. He just kept those feelings to himself. It felt safer that way.

By Monday, Kelsey realized she had run out of people to interview. She had read all the police reports and made copies of some, which she had highlighted and underlined. She had compiled a database in her computer, with a list of everyone she had talked to and everything they had told her. She had created a rough timeline of Liz's life between the time she'd left Iowa and the time she had disappeared. The only information she had gathered that wasn't already in the police reports was that Liz had said she was meeting someone outside the ice cream parlor a few weeks before she went missing. But no one had seen the man or the meeting.

Kelsey decided to go back to the newspaper office. This time, she was looking for news items in the year before Liz's arrival in town—any stories about young women, newly arrived in town, who'd been assaulted or had fights with a boyfriend. She knew there had been no murders reported in the county in the decades prior to Liz's death—a fact that had been stated both in an article in the paper about Liz's murder and in one of the reports in her file.

It was a very long shot, but Kelsey was betting that the man who had killed Liz might have tried with someone else before. Maybe Liz wasn't the first young woman he had lured to town, but that woman had gotten away.

Yet hours of paging through the heavy volumes of back issues yielded only a pounding head and ink-stained fingers.

The door to the morgue opened, and Tammy Patterson stepped in. Her curly hair was in a messy bun today, a pen stuck through the topknot. "How's it going?" she asked.

"Not that well," Kelsey admitted. She closed the volume she'd had open before her. "The truth is, I've read everything you have here, and I'm not finding what I need. I don't know where to look."

Tammy sat in the chair across from Kelsey. "You're looking for information about your sister's murder, right? Elizabeth Chapman?"

Kelsey nodded. "Are you familiar with the story?"

"I looked it up after you were here the first time. Such a tragedy."

"There are so many things I don't know," Kelsey said. "I was hoping by coming here, I could fill in at least a few of the blanks."

"What if I wrote a story about your search?"

"You mean, a newspaper story?"

"It's what I do. And I think it's interesting." She swept her hand in front of her at eye level as if underlining a headline. "'A Sister's Search for Justice.'" She grinned. "That sounds good, doesn't it?"

"I don't know," Kelsey said. Being written about in the paper felt so...exposed.

"It would be a great way to get the case back in the public eye again," Tammy said. "Someone might come forward with new evidence. If there are any specific things you want to know, we could ask people to contact you. Someone might have seen something and not even know its significance. For all the newcomers we have in town, there are still a lot of people who live here now who were living in Eagle Mountain back then."

Tammy's enthusiasm was infectious, and hope flared in Kelsey again. "All right," she said. "When do you want to interview me?"

"How about right now?" Tammy pulled a notebook from her pocket. "We've got space in the next issue."

Chapter Ten

Tony was surprised to get a call from Jessica MacIntosh Monday morning. He was surveying a utility right-of-way and moved into the shade of a pinyon tree to answer his phone.

"Hey, Tony," Jessica said. "Is your friend still in town—Liz's sister?"

"Kelsey is still here." At least, he assumed she was. She hadn't contacted him to say goodbye, and she struck him as the type who would.

"Talking with her got Andy and me thinking about Liz and what happened to her."

Tony removed his straw hat and wiped the sweat from his brow. Even on a cool spring day like this, the sun was intense. "Did you remember something?" he asked.

"No, but I did some digging, and I found Ben Everett."

"The guy who wanted to date Liz?"

"Yeah. He's living in Junction now—can you

believe it? He just moved back to the area. I told him about Kelsey, and he wants to talk to her."

"That's great."

"Let me give you his number and you can pass it on to Kelsey, okay?"

"Sure. Let me get something to write with." He found a pen and jotted down the number on the back of a gas receipt he found in his pocket. "Thanks a lot, Jessica."

"I don't know if it will help, but at least it's something, right?"

"At least it's something," he repeated as he tucked away his phone once more. Ben probably didn't know any more than anyone else, but the more people Tony found for Kelsey to talk to, the longer she would stay in town. He knew she would leave eventually, but while she was around, his life felt better.

KELSEY WALKED BACK to the Alpiner Inn Monday afternoon after her interview with Tammy Patterson and was surprised to find Tony waiting for her. "Tony, it's so good to see you," she said, and impulsively embraced him. It was like hugging a stone statue, until he relaxed a little and returned the embrace.

"It's good to see you, too," he said.

"I was just interviewed for the paper," she said. "Tammy Patterson is going to write an article about my search for Mountain Man and information about Liz's life here. We're hoping someone who remembers something will read the article and contact me. Isn't that a good idea?"

"I guess so."

"You guess so?" She frowned. "Do you think it was a bad idea?"

"It's a good idea," he said. "As long as the killer doesn't see it and decide to come after you."

She stared at him, a little light-headed at the thought. He grabbed her elbow. "I shouldn't have said that. I'm sorry. I'm sure it will be fine. Just...promise you'll be careful."

His genuine concern touched her. How long had it been since anyone had cared about her that much? Her mother was trying, but long years of indifference had carved deep grooves in their lives that were hard to steer out of.

"I promise I'll be careful," she said. "So, what brings you my way this afternoon?"

"I have Ben Everett's contact information. He wants to talk to you about Liz."

Some of her tension eased. "That's wonderful! Where is he? How did you find him?"

"I can't take credit. Jessica found him. He's in Junction."

"And that's near here?" she asked, unsure.

"It's about an hour from here."

"And he wants to talk to me. That's fantastic." She grabbed his arm. "Will you go with me to see him? I know you're really busy, but I would love to have you with me."

"I'll go with you. As long as I don't get a call-out from Search and Rescue." It was probably the first time in his life he had wished for no calls at all on that date.

"When can you go?" she asked.

"Why don't you call him and set something up?" he said. "As long as it's after five or on a weekend, I should be available." He handed her the piece of paper with Ben's number.

"I'm going to call him right now." She pulled out her phone and punched in the number. She listened to a message telling her that Ben Everett was unable to come to the phone, then said, "This is Kelsey Chapman. I'm looking for information about my sister, Liz, and I understand you knew her in high school. Please call me so we can set up a time for me to come to Junction and we can talk." She left her number and ended the call.

"What are you going to do now?" Tony asked.

"Are you tired of having dinner with me?"

He shook his head. "No."

She took his hand again. He had rough hands,

calloused and strong. She liked the feel of them against her skin. "I was hoping you'd say that," she said.

KELSEY AND TONY stayed late at the restaurant, talking about their college experiences—neither of them was a big joiner, but they had branched out a little and made friends. "I felt more normal in college," she said. "Though I was still aware that I was different from my classmates. They had parents who visited the campus and families they looked forward to seeing at the holidays."

"I only attended school for two more years after high school," Tony said. "That's all I needed to get my surveyor's license, and I wanted to come back to Eagle Mountain and work search and rescue."

"Is your brother still here?" she asked.

"He moved while I was away at school." He smiled, a rueful look. "It didn't matter. I'd already decided I wasn't going to live with him when I got back."

"Do you still see him?"

"Sometimes. He's in Denver. Our lives are so different."

She nodded. She had spent much of her life trying to figure out how to get past the differences that separated her from other people. "But your nephew is still here, right? Chris?"

Tony nodded. "He just showed up on my doorstep a few days ago and asked if he could stay." He sat back, one leg stretched out in front of him, as if he was trying to get comfortable. "He pointed out that since his dad had taken me in when I was a teenager, the least I could do was return the favor. I couldn't argue with that."

"How old is Chris?"

"He's twenty-three. Probably almost twenty-four."

"And he just decided to move back to his old home town?" She sensed Tony wasn't going to offer any details if she didn't ask.

Tony let out a long sigh, and she wondered if she had pushed too far. She was about to say it was really none of her business when he said, "He got in a little trouble back in Denver and needed somewhere to make a fresh start."

"That was good of you to take him in. How's the arrangement working out?" From what she had seen, Tony's house was small, and he struck her as a very private person. Adding a roommate couldn't have been easy.

"It's okay." Tony shook his head. "He's a lot different from me at his age. He got the job at Mo's right away, but he doesn't seem to have any idea what he wants to do with his life."

"You had a plan for your life right out of high

school," she said. "It took me forever to figure out what I wanted to do."

"You didn't always want to be an accountant?" Now his smile was genuine—teasing, with a little heat behind it.

"I didn't even like math in school." She laughed. "But it's a good job. I don't dislike it."

"And when you're not working?" he asked. "What do you like to do?"

She thought for a moment. She didn't have any real hobbies, like painting or knitting. She didn't play any sports. "I like to read," she said. "And I like walking. Taking long walks in parks or through towns. I've enjoyed the walks I've taken here."

"If you like hiking, this is the place to be," he said. "There are hundreds of miles of trails in the mountains."

"It would be fun to explore them. With the right guide." She met his gaze and felt the tension between them. The wanting. She sensed he was like her—someone who had spent so many years craving an intimacy that had been denied them. Only now, with him, that kind of closeness felt almost within reach.

He was the first to look away. "How long are you staying in town?" he asked.

"I don't know." She had the room for another week, but would it be so bad to stay longer? To explore those trails and wait for the wildflowers to bloom? To get to know Tony better?

The clatter of glasses startled her out of her reverie. Who was she kidding? If anyone was a confirmed loner, it was Tony. She was pretty sure he was attracted to her, too, but when she went back to Iowa, he would probably settle back into his regular life without a ripple of concern.

"What's your favorite hike in the area?" she asked, steering the conversation into safer territory. Sharing her deepest thoughts and emotions with him had felt liberating, but it also made her vulnerable. She wanted to drop her guard and trust him, but doing so with other people had burned her badly before.

They talked until closing time yet again, then he walked her back to the inn. Eagle Mountain was dark and silent; every business was closed, and no cars were on the street. They walked close together, not touching, but she could feel the warmth of his body. She'd just opened her mouth to say something about how beautiful the night was when the screech of tires jolted a cry from her.

She turned, only to be bombarded by bright headlights. Tony grabbed her arm and jerked her off her feet, pulling her with him as the vehicle raced past, veering onto the sidewalk before roaring into the night.

She clung to Tony, and the two of them huddled against the cold brick of a closed art gallery, hearts pounding painfully. She could hear the drumbeat of his pulse against her ear—her head pressed to his neck, both his arms wrapped tightly around her. She closed her eyes and listened to that steady rhythm, willing herself to breathe evenly, to calm down.

"What was wrong with that guy?" she asked after a while. "Was he drunk or something?"

"I don't know." He loosened his hold on her and pulled away enough to look at her. The streetlight on the corner cast long shadows across his face, hiding his eyes, but she heard the concern in his voice. "Are you okay?"

"I'm fine." She pushed herself upright but kept her hands on his chest. "How could he not see us? We were almost under the streetlight."

"Maybe he did see us," Tony said.

A few seconds passed before the meaning behind his words hit her. "You think he ran us down on purpose?" She was having trouble breathing again, panic rising.

"I don't know." He tightened his hold once more.

She looked in the direction the car had disappeared. "Could you tell what kind of car it was?" she asked. "The engine was so loud. It sounded big."

"I think it might have been a truck. But he had his lights on bright. I couldn't really see anything." His voice shook with emotion. "I'm just glad you're all right."

"I'm all right." She slid one hand up to the back of his neck. "I'm all right because I'm with you." Then she stood on tiptoe and pressed her lips to his, kissing him as if this was the last chance for a kiss she would ever have.

He returned the kiss with the same fervor; his lips warm, assured. His beard was soft against her cheek, and he smelled like soap and pine and something indefinable she could only identify as *him*. As reserved as he might be at times, he held nothing back with this kiss. He was ardent yet tender. This wasn't the sloppy, demanding kisses of her college hookups or the hard, almost-mechanical passion of the men who assumed she wanted the quick release they sought. Tony's kisses made her feel cherished. Desired not for what she could give but for herself. Maybe he didn't have words to express how he felt, but he was showing her now. He slid his hands beneath her coat and caressed her hips. She arched to him, his hard arousal pressed against her sending a rush of heat through her. She wanted to wrap her legs around him, oblivious to their surroundings. “Tony!” she gasped when he finally released her mouth.

He pulled back as if scorched. “Did I hurt you?” he asked.

“No!” She cupped his face and stared into his eyes. “You could never hurt me,” she said.

She wanted him to kiss her again—to keep kissing her for the rest of the night—but he turned away. “It’s cold,” he said. “I’d better get you back to the inn.”

But he kept hold of her hand as they walked, fingers entwined, and when she raised his knuckles to her lips, he didn’t protest. They stopped outside the inn, and she wanted to ask him in. He must have sensed what she was thinking because he said, “It would be awkward if the Richardses found me here in the morning.”

She nodded. This was still a small town. These people were his friends, and she was a stranger. An outsider. Again. “Good night,” she said, and stood on tiptoe to kiss him once more. Tenderly, a brush of her mouth to his that still left her trembling as she turned and walked away from him.

Chapter Eleven

Tony left the inn, but he didn't go home. Instead, he retraced their route, then drove in the direction the vehicle that had almost hit them had taken. He didn't know what he expected to find, but he was too restless to settle for the night. His heart raced with desire and anxiety and the knowledge of how close he had come to losing Kelsey. The memory of those headlights bearing down on them left him shaking.

He spotted a vehicle pulled over to the side of the road up ahead—a Rayford County Sheriff's Department SUV. He flashed his lights, then pulled over in front of the vehicle and cut the engine. Deputy Jake Gwynn got out and met him between the vehicles. "What are you doing out so late, Tony?" Jake asked.

Jake's schedule at the sheriff's department limited his availability for callouts. "How long have you been sitting here?" Tony asked.

"About half an hour," Jake said. "It's a good

place to catch drunk drivers on their way out of town and catch up on paperwork."

"You stop anybody while you've been here?"

"No. It's been a quiet night. Why are you asking?"

"Kelsey Chapman and I were walking from the Cakewalk Café to the Alpiner tonight, and someone almost ran us over. The vehicle came up on the sidewalk and must have been doing forty, at least. I don't know how we weren't killed." His heart raced again at the memory.

"What kind of vehicle?" Jake asked. "Did you get a plate number? Or a look at the driver?"

Tony shook his head. "He had his brights on. And he raced away so fast we couldn't see anything."

"Are you okay?"

Tony nodded. "Shook up but okay."

"A few people have driven by me but none of them speeding or driving erratically," Jake said. "Do you want to file a report?"

Tony shoved his hands into his jacket pockets. The wind had picked up, and he was cold. Probably the adrenaline draining off. "What would be the point? I was just hoping you'd seen someone."

"Sorry I couldn't help." Jake assumed a more casual stance, leaning against the front fender of his SUV. "So, you and Kelsey Chapman," he said. "She seems really nice."

"She is." He braced himself for some comment about Kelsey being so much younger than him, or her being from out of town, or even the observation that he didn't usually date.

Instead, Jake said, "Do you think what happened tonight had anything to do with all the questions she's been asking about her sister's murder?"

Tony nodded. "I wondered. If the killer is still around, he probably heard about her and isn't too happy. He's gotten away with murder for twenty years."

"Has anything else like this happened?" Jake asked. "Any threats or unexplained accidents?"

"Not that she's mentioned." But she might not. Tony was learning she could be as reserved as he was.

"Let me know if anything else happens," Jake said.

"I will." He walked back to his Toyota and turned it around, heading back toward his house. Jake had given voice to the suspicions he had been trying to ignore—that a killer had targeted Kelsey.

The idea panicked him, but panic wasn't going to solve anything. He gripped the steering wheel more tightly and focused instead on the sensation of Kelsey's body against his, the scent of her surrounding him, the heat of her warming places that had been cold for so long. Leaving her just now had been one of the hardest things he had ever done, but he'd had to go. Mistakes happened when he acted without thinking. Some people thrived on spontaneity and following their desires, but those were the people he pulled off ledges or rescued from the wilderness when they were lost. Logic and planning didn't solve every problem, but it prevented a lot of them.

There was nothing logical about his feelings for Kelsey, though. She was young and beautiful, and she never looked at him as if he was odd or awkward or all the things he knew others saw. She had *wanted* him tonight, and that in itself was a gift. But what would happen if he took that gift? She was going to leave, probably sooner rather than later. All his life, people had been leaving him, and strong as he tried to be, he didn't think he could take having Kelsey, only to lose her, too.

TUESDAY MORNING, Kelsey woke gasping for breath, heart pounding painfully. She put a hand to her chest and stared at the sun streaming in the window, the memory of the dream that had wakened her slow to recede. Her eyes burned from the glare of headlights coming toward her, the roar of an engine blocking all other sound. She focused on breathing deeply, reminding herself that she was okay. She was alive. She was safe.

She shifted her thoughts to the aftermath of those frightening moments on the sidewalk—she and Tony kissing, finally giving vent to the passion that had simmered between them for days. If he had stayed with her last night, she was sure she wouldn't have dreamed of that racing vehicle.

She thought about calling him but resisted the urge. He struck her as a man who needed space. She didn't want to push him away by being too clingy.

She didn't want to ask for more than he was ready to give. He hadn't been faking his feelings for her last night—she was sure. She would be patient and allow things to develop between them naturally.

Gradually, her heartbeat calmed and she was able to breathe normally. She sat up and checked the clock. It was almost seven o'clock. She would shower, get dressed, go down to breakfast and decide how to spend the rest of the day. Ben Everett should call her back today. If he didn't, she would call him.

She set about these tasks, but she couldn't

completely shake the dream—which had, after all, only been a replay of terrifying reality. She tried to tell herself it had been a careless driver, maybe someone looking at their cell phone instead of paying attention to the road.

But the memory of that growling engine, the vehicle accelerating as it came up onto the sidewalk, sent a shudder through her. A distracted driver would have looked up the moment his tire hit the curb, and every instinct would have been to brake. This driver hadn't braked.

But who would want to deliberately hurt them?

Liz's killer. The thought ought to have frightened her, but perversely, a thrill raced through her. If that driver was the person who had murdered Liz, that meant he was here in Eagle Mountain. And she was close enough to identifying him to make him worried.

Maybe he was trying to scare her off, but he only made her more determined to keep digging. Every bit of new information she gathered brought her closer to discovering his identity and finding justice for Liz—and a little peace for her family.

TONY WOKE EARLY TUESDAY, his first thoughts of Liz and everything that had happened last night. Was she all right? He wanted to urge her again to be careful, that he didn't think that vehicle almost hitting them had been an accident. All those questions she had been asking about Liz's murder must be making someone uncomfortable. He knew she wanted to find Liz's killer, and he believed Liz deserved that justice. Her murderer should be punished.

But not if it meant Kelsey getting hurt. He reached for his phone on the nightstand, then pulled back. He had no claim on Kelsey. No right to suggest she act one way or another. If he called her, she might think he was going too far—pressuring her, even.

He set the phone aside, pulled on pants and headed for the kitchen to start coffee. As he passed through the living room, he looked toward the sofa, relieved to see the familiar lump of blankets, one pale foot uncovered. So Chris had made it home last night.

He turned toward the kitchen and almost collided with a woman with a mop of dark curls, long bare legs showing beneath the hem of the T-shirt that appeared to be the only thing she was wearing. He stumbled back and made some incoherent noise.

She smiled. "Hi. You must be Uncle Tony. I'm Amy."

Tony glanced over his shoulder toward the

sofa. It was either that or continue staring at her. "You're a, um, friend of Chris's?" he asked.

"Yeah. I went ahead and started coffee. I hope you don't mind. It should be ready in a few."

"No. I mean, thanks. I'll, uh, just get dressed." He retreated to the bedroom to put on the rest of his clothes and hoped she would take the hint to do the same.

When he emerged from the bathroom after a quick shower ten minutes later, he found Chris and Amy, both dressed in jeans and T-shirts, giggling over coffee at the kitchen table while Chris dropped frozen waffles into the toaster. "Hey, Tony," Chris said. "Amy says you two met."

"We did." He filled a mug from the coffee carafe, noting there was just enough left for one cup.

"Chris told me how you were part of the Search and Rescue crew that hauled him up out of the canyon when Blake Russell's Jeep went over the edge Sunday," Amy said.

Tony nodded.

"Blake said the car is trashed," Chris said. "He's hoping the insurance pays enough to get a new one. He's thinking a truck this time."

"I'd get the exact same model of car," Amy said. "After all, that one survived the crash, and both of you lived to tell the tale."

"It was a wild ride," Chris said. "I wish now I'd taken the time to appreciate it."

"Did your life flash before your eyes like they say happens?" Amy asked.

"Nah. All I could think was that I sure wasn't going to ask Blake for a ride again."

They were still laughing as Tony left for work.

He was unlocking his truck when Chris ran up to him. "Hey," he said, stopping beside Tony.

"Hey, yourself." Tony opened the door of his truck.

"You're not upset about Amy, are you? About me bringing her back here last night?"

"I'm not upset." It was unsettling, having yet another person—a stranger—in the home that had been his alone for so long, but he remembered what it was like to be Chris's age. Or at least, he remembered what it had been like for him. "I want you to feel like this is your home. But it might have been a little awkward if I had walked in on you two last night."

Chris shoved his hands into the front pockets of his knit joggers. "Yeah, well, she still lives with her parents, so that's not an option." He grinned. "Maybe we should work out some kind of signal or something, like a rag tied to the doorknob or a window shade pulled down halfway—in case you have a lady friend over sometime and need privacy."

Tony started to say that wasn't going to happen, but he stopped himself. He had come close to asking Kelsey to come back here with him last night. The thought of possibly encountering Chris had kept him from extending the invitation, but obviously, his nephew wasn't a naive kid anymore. "We'll think of something," he said. "Though something tied to the doorknob or a window shade isn't going to do any good if you come home after I'm in bed alone."

"We obviously didn't wake you," Chris said. "And anyway, I knew you were sound asleep. You snore like a grizzly bear. We could hear you all the way in the living room."

Laughing, he turned away. Tony smiled and slid into the truck. He liked that after all that had happened in his young life, Chris could still laugh so easily.

BEN EVERETT RETURNED Kelsey's call midday on Tuesday, and they arranged to meet at six thirty that evening at his home in Junction. As soon as she ended the call with him, she phoned Tony. "Hey," he said. "I'm driving to a job site, so you're on the speaker in the car. My helper, Brad, is with me."

"Hello," a male voice said.

Kelsey had intended to say something flirtatious and maybe even a little risqué but thought better of it. "Ben can meet us this evening at six thirty at his house," she said. "Will that work for you?"

"I'll pick you up at five thirty," he said.

"Great. See you then."

She started to end the call, but he asked, "What are you doing today?"

"I'm going to review all my notes, maybe make some calls related to work," she said. "And I need to think about what I want to ask Ben."

"That's good," he said. "If you go out, be careful."

The concern she heard behind the words touched her. "I will," she said.

"See you at five thirty," he said, and ended the call.

She lay back on the bed and stared at the ceiling, the memory of kissing him last night coming back to her, every sensation so vivid it was almost as if he were still touching her. The intensity of her feelings frightened her. She wasn't like this. When other people panicked, she was calm. It wasn't that she didn't feel things, but she didn't let those emotions show. She didn't want to be that vulnerable.

But Tony had stripped away every pretense.

Every nerve felt exposed to him, and it was both painful and exhilarating. And none of it made sense. She had come here to learn about her sister. Not to discover this hidden side of herself.

Ben Everett lived in a very modern steel-and-glass home perched on the side of a canyon in a neighborhood full of similar modern homes on the west side of Junction. Tony pulled his Toyota into the driveway as the sun was setting and turning the expansive windows the deep oranges and pinks of saltwater taffy. Ben came to the door as they walked up a stone path—a slender man with swept-back blond hair, dressed in running shoes, gray slacks and a white polo. "Ben Everett," he said, and offered a firm handshake.

Kelsey introduced herself, then turned to Tony. "I remember you," Ben said, clapping Tony on the shoulder. "It's good to see you again."

"It's good to see you, too," Tony said. Ben's claim to remember him seemed sincere, but it surprised him. Though their high school class had been small, the two of them hadn't moved in the same circles, and Tony, having been new to the group, had always been on the edges of any activity, on the outside looking in. Ben had been handsome, athletic and popular—the one boy with enough confidence to pursue Liz Chapman.

Ben led them into a great room with soaring ceilings and a wall of glass that looked out into the canyon, the dying sun bathing its sides in watercolor shades. Whatever he did for a living now, he had obviously done well financially. "Can I get you a drink or anything to eat?" he asked.

"No, thank you," Kelsey said, and settled onto a long brown suede sofa. Tony sat beside her and had the sensation of sinking into a marshmallow. Kelsey brushed her hand against his thigh and smiled as if grateful to have him near.

"My wife took the kids to soccer, so we have the place to ourselves for a couple of hours," Ben said, sinking into the chair across from them. He studied Kelsey a moment. "I can see the resemblance to your sister."

It was true that Kelsey and Liz had the same coloring and the same dimple on the left side of the mouth. But Tony saw all the ways she was different from her sister. Kelsey had none of the boldness that had made Liz both fascinating and forbidding. Kelsey was quieter and more contemplative. More introverted. More like him.

"Did you know Liz well?" she asked Ben.

"If you had asked me that back in high school, I would have said yes." He laced his fingers together over one knee. "She and I were friends. I wanted more, but she made it clear that wasn't possible."

Kelsey leaned forward, hope written so clearly in her expression. "When you say *friends*, do you mean she confided in you?"

"She did and she didn't." He tilted his head. "I'm sure you've already talked to enough people to know that after she disappeared, we found out a lot of things she hadn't told us. I had no idea she wasn't living with her parents. She said she had moved to Eagle Mountain from Iowa, and I just assumed she meant her whole family had moved."

"Did she ever mention a boyfriend?" Kelsey asked.

"Yes."

Kelsey fumbled her pen. "She did? Did she tell you his name?"

"She did not." He cracked his knuckles. "Why don't I start at the beginning, tell you what I know and you can ask questions to fill in the blanks. Though there are a lot of things I don't know."

"Yes, please." Kelsey laid down her pen and sat back, though Tony could feel the slight tremble that ran through her. He reached over and took her hand; she didn't pull away. "Tell me everything," she said.

Chapter Twelve

Twenty years ago

"Liz, I know you like me. Why won't you go to the prom with me?" Ben leaned against the locker next to Liz's and watched her rummage through the chaos inside, searching for who knew what. Liz was smart and beautiful and sharp as a razor—but organized, she was not.

"I can't go with you, Ben," she said. "But it's really sweet of you to ask."

Sweet was for little girls and puppy dogs. He didn't want Liz to think of him as sweet. "Are you going with someone else?" he asked. "You can tell me. I promise I won't get angry." Jealous as hell, but that was nothing new. Every guy in school lusted after Liz; it was a known fact.

"I'm not going with anyone else." She closed the locker and turned to face him. "I'm not going to prom."

"But why not?" He straightened. "It's the last

big party before graduation. The prom committee goes all out to make it special."

She shook her head. "I'm not going."

"It won't be the same without you." He leaned closer, his voice low. "Is it a money thing? Because I could help you with the dress and stuff." Ben's parents had money, and they were generous with him and his sister.

She touched his shoulder, and his knees almost buckled. "That's so sweet, but no, it's not because of money." She moved past him, heading toward the exit doors. He lengthened his stride to catch up with her.

"I'm not going to leave you alone until you tell me why you can't go," he said.

She looked around them, as if checking for anyone who might be listening. They exited the doors, and she pulled him to one side, into an alcove behind what was supposed to be a native-plant garden but was mostly a circle of dirt with some rocks. "You have to swear to never tell a soul," she said.

"I swear," he said, excited by the prospect of sharing a secret with her.

She looked into his eyes, hers so blue—and a little sad. "I mean it. Not a word to anyone."

He nodded. "Okay."

She took a deep breath and let it out. "I can't

go with you because I'm already seeing someone," she said.

"You're kidding." It wasn't the mature, reasonable response he wanted to make, but the words burst out before he could take them back.

"I'm not kidding." She smoothed her hands down her arms. "He's older, and he's really jealous."

"I've never seen you in town with anyone else," he said. Was she trying to spare his feelings or shake him off by making up this older guy?

"We have to keep our relationship secret," she said.

"Why? That's messed up."

She smiled, but her eyes still held that sad look.

"Who is this guy?" he asked. "How did you meet him?"

"I met him online," she said. "And you don't need to know his name."

He knotted his fists, beyond frustrated with this mystery game she insisted on playing. "Why do you want to hang out with some older guy?" he asked. He knew it was a pointless question. Girls always wanted older guys. Older guys had cool cars and money and experience with sex. He drove a Toyota, had an allowance and had slept with one girl, someone he had met over Christmas break on vacation in Vail. She had been nice, but they hadn't even talked since.

Liz put her hand on his arm again. She must have thought she was being kind; she didn't realize she was torturing him. "If I was going to go to prom, I would go with you," she said. "I have to go now. But remember—you swore not to tell anyone my secret."

"I won't tell." She left and he told himself he wasn't going to turn around and watch her like some lovesick fool. But he could only stare at the ground for a few seconds before he did turn and look after her. Her long brown hair swayed in counterpoint to her hips as she walked, graceful and almost not real.

"Why didn't you tell the sheriff about this older boyfriend?" Kelsey asked when Ben had finished his story. He had confirmed what she already believed—that Liz had moved to Eagle Mountain to be with Mountain Man. But if he had told the sheriff about this jealous boyfriend, they might have done more to try to find him right away.

"I had promised her I wouldn't say anything." Ben blew out a breath. "And the cops didn't ask. If they had, I probably would have caved and told them everything. I was scared spitless when they hauled me into the station. They accused me of killing her. They said I was angry because she wouldn't go out with me. I would have told them anything they wanted to know, but they didn't ask." He shook his head. "I thought I was being honorable, keeping her secret. I was just a kid. I know better now."

"You must have been watching her after that," Tony said. "Did you ever see her with anyone?"

Kelsey nodded, grateful he had thought to ask this question.

"Yeah, I watched her. You did, too. I saw you. I saw how all the guys looked at her, and it made me feel kind of hopeless. I was so gone over her, and I know to her, I was just a nice boy." He said the word *boy* as if it was a curse. "I never saw her with anyone but friends at school. Girlfriends. I even tried following her home one day, but she saw me and told me to leave her alone. She acted so hurt I had to go. I didn't want her to think I was some kind of creep." He turned back to Kelsey. "Do you think this boyfriend is the one who killed her?"

"I don't know," Kelsey said. "But if I could find him, the sheriff could compare his DNA to the evidence he still has."

"They took my DNA," Ben said. "I had nightmares afterwards that I had somehow left DNA on her clothes when I brushed against her or something, but it turned out I wasn't a match. What kind of evidence do they have? I never heard."

"They have skin cells from under the fingernails," Kelsey said. "They think she fought with her attacker."

"I hope she scarred him for life," he said. He stood and began to pace. "I was wrecked when I found out she was dead. I felt guilty, as if I could have saved her. That was foolish, too, but that's how kids are sometimes. Everything is all about you at that age." He stopped in front of Kelsey. "Do you know anything about this guy—the boyfriend?"

"She told you the truth when she said she met him online. There are copies of some of the emails they exchanged in the case file. He signed his messages Mountain Man, and that's how she referred to him with us. She refused to tell us his name. She told my parents she was going to Colorado to be with him, and then she left."

"Your parents must have been worried sick," Ben said.

"They were," Kelsey agreed. "But she was eighteen. My dad said if she wanted to leave, there wasn't anything he could do to stop her. He was sure she would come home after a few weeks."

Ben sat once more and leaned forward, elbows on his knees, head bowed. She pictured him as a good-looking yet awkward teen—almost a man but still a boy, too. In love with her sister, whom everyone seemed to adore.

Everyone but her killer.

"When they found her body, it broke something in me," Ben continued. He looked up, face anguished. "It broke something in all of us. I mean, none of us were old enough to have experienced real tragedy. And we thought we knew Liz. She was our friend. But then we found out how much we didn't know about her."

"Is there anything else you remember about Liz?" Kelsey asked. "Anything at all that might help?"

"I've thought and thought, but I really can't. When she first disappeared, I thought maybe she had moved and just not told all of us. Maybe her dad got transferred or something. Then one of her teachers asked me if I knew where she was. That's when I got really worried. That's when I first realized how much she hadn't told me about herself. I didn't know her parents' names or where she lived or anything. Then, when they found her body like that..." He shook his head. "At first, we all thought she must have fallen hiking and hit her head. It would still have been terrible, but those kinds of accidents happen. The first time I heard she had been murdered was when the sheriff's deputies brought me in for questioning and accused me of having killed her." He looked at Tony. "Did you know when you found her? Did you know she had been murdered?"

"No," Tony said. "I thought it was an accident, too." He cleared his throat. "The deputies tried to get me to confess to killing her, too."

Ben nodded. "I guess they were desperate to find the murderer, and since the evidence wasn't pointing to anyone in particular, they decided to try to pressure a confession out of every guy who'd ever been near her."

"Who else did they accuse?" Kelsey asked. "Do you know?"

Ben and Tony exchanged glances, then Ben shook his head. "I don't know who else they accused. I just know they never found the person who did that to her."

They sat in silence with this thought, then Kelsey gathered her notebook and purse and stood. "Thank you for talking with me," she said. "You're the first person to confirm there actually was a boyfriend, and I appreciate that."

"I hope it helps." He walked with them to the door. "I guess the boyfriend is the most likely suspect, but what if it wasn't him? What if it was just some random killer?"

"If that's the case, we'll probably never know," she said.

"Will you let me know if you find out anything?"

"I will."

They said goodbye and left. "That was intense," Tony said as he started the car.

"Yes." She blew out a breath. "But it was good to hear someone confirm that Mountain Man existed. If he was real, we ought to be able to find him."

"If anything happens to me, I hope I have someone like you on my side," he said. "You never give up."

"Neither do you." She angled her body toward him. "Think how many people would have died in these mountains if you and the rest of the Search and Rescue volunteers had given up."

"That was a matter of life or death," he said.

"This feels like that, too."

He nodded. "I guess it does." He smoothed his hands along the steering wheel. "So what next?"

"Let's go back to your place."

"You want to see where I live?"

"I want to finish what we started last night."

To his credit, he didn't falter, though she thought he turned a shade paler. "Are you sure that's a good idea?" he asked.

She leaned over and put a hand on his thigh. "I think it's a very good idea."

He cleared his throat. "If you're leaving town—"

"Shh. I know you're not afraid of risks. You risk everything every time you go out on a search and rescue call. Don't be afraid to take a chance on me. On us."

Chapter Thirteen

Tony knew all about being afraid and moving forward anyway. He wasn't afraid of Kelsey, of course—only of making a mistake. But he wasn't going to let that fear stop him from savoring this moment. He pulled into the driveway of his home and stopped the car. A quick glance showed no sign of Chris's motorcycle. It was only a few minutes after nine, and he seldom made it in before ten.

"Is your nephew home?" Kelsey asked, as if reading his mind.

"I'm pretty sure he's out." He gestured toward the front of the garage, where a security light cast a warm circle of light on the front of the house. "He parks his motorcycle there."

He got out of the car and wondered if he should walk around to open her door, but she slid out and met him at the front of the vehicle. They were halfway up the walk to the front door when she stopped and looked up at the house. "I like it," she said. "It looks like you."

"You've lost me there. How am I like a house? Or how is my house like me?"

"You're both simple yet handsome, strong and unpretentious. And you look like you belong in the mountains."

He laughed. "I'm not handsome."

She slid her arm around him. "You are to me."

He was half-afraid she was trying to flatter him, but he reminded himself she wasn't like that. He unlocked the door and let her in. He had brought women to this place before, but it had been a long time. And he had never wanted to impress them the way he wanted to impress Kelsey. "Welcome," he said, and tossed his keys onto the table by the door.

"It's beautiful," she said.

He knew her words were true because, unlike him, the house *was* beautiful. He had worked hard to make it so, replacing the old, narrow casements with larger picture windows, refinishing all the woodwork to a warm cherry hue, installing a tiled woodburning stove and sanding the wide pine floors to restore them to their original patina. The furniture was simple, mostly leather and wood. Comfortable.

"Chris, are you here?" he called. The bike

hadn't been in the driveway, but there was always the chance that it had broken down and Chris had gotten a ride home from a friend.

No answer. Good. They were alone.

He watched Kelsey while she examined the house. She walked around the room, studying the books on the shelves; examining a coaster made of a wood round cut from a length of firewood; admiring the prints on the wall, most of them by local artists, purchased at fundraising events for the Search and Rescue team. He was still standing there when she turned and walked into his arms. "Thank you for bringing me here," she said. "For letting me invade your sanctuary."

"I'm happy to have you here." He kissed her. Not the desperate flood of passion like last night but a more deliberate caress, enjoying the sensation of her satin lips, her tongue sending sparks of desire through him as it tangled with his.

She slid her hands underneath his shirt and moaned. "You don't know how much I've wanted to do this," she whispered, her mouth against his neck.

"I think I have an idea." He put his hand over hers, stopping the tantalizing progress of her fingers up his body. "Give me a sec, okay?"

"Okay." Looking amused, she watched as he glanced around the room until he spotted a dish towel on the corner of the bar. He grabbed it, then returned to the front door and knotted the towel around the doorknob, where it would be clearly visible to anyone approaching. By the time he returned to her, she was trying to stifle a giggle. "Was that a…a signal?" she asked, laughter escaping from behind the hand that covered her mouth.

"I don't want any interruptions," he said. "Do you?"

She shook her head. He grabbed the hem of his T-shirt, pulled it off over his head and tossed it across the room. The soft look in her eyes made him feel unsteady on his feet, and when she reached out and traced her fingers along the knotted muscles of his shoulders, he suppressed a groan.

She stopped at the thick ridge of scar tissue across the top of his left shoulder. "What is this?" she asked, voice full of concern.

"I had an accident last winter," he said.

"What happened?"

He took her hand and led her toward the bedroom. "Come in here and I'll show you." She might as well know what she was getting into before they went too far. His body had a story to tell, and it wasn't always pretty.

The bedroom was a smaller space at the back of the house, with an antique bed, a nightstand

and a single chair where he dumped his clothes before they made it into the hamper. He stood beside the chair now and began to undress as she watched from the doorway. He wasn't embarrassed or self-conscious. Months of surgeries and hospital stays and grueling rehab had erased any remnants of modesty he might once have possessed.

He only cringed when he heard her small gasp. He knew the scars were ugly—white and recessed or red and raised. They were fading and would fade more as time passed, but they marked him and reminded him of how close he had walked to death.

He didn't hear her cross the room, but suddenly, she was beside him, reaching out to touch each scar, then bending to kiss the one on his chest, where they had inserted a tube to reinflate his collapsed lung. She bent lower, to the place where doctors had repaired his broken pelvis with metal screws and plates. Down farther, to the crisscross of scars on his right leg, broken in three places by the fall. Her hot breath against his skin made him shiver, and his erection was almost painful in its intensity.

He touched her shoulder and urged her to her feet again. "Come here," he said, and she moved closer.

She didn't make a move to remove her clothes

but let him undress her. Unlike him, she was perfect, her skin creamy and unblemished, small round breasts tipped with pink nipples, a gentle curve of waist to hips and thighs poets would probably write odes to. All he could do was run his hands over her and curse the roughness of the calluses built up from many years of climbing.

She slipped her hand into his and kissed his shoulder. "Take me to bed, and tell me your story," she said.

There was no point asking if she still wanted him now that she had seen him. Clearly, she did. And he had never wanted anything as badly as he wanted her. But he forced himself to wait a little longer. Long enough to tell her. "I was descending into a canyon during a search and rescue training exercise," he said. "My ropes gave way and I fell."

She made a choking sound and pressed a hand to his chest. He covered her hand with his own, then lifted it to his mouth and kissed her fingers. "One of the other volunteers had burned the ropes with acid so that they broke when I was halfway down."

"He hated you that much?" she asked.

"He didn't hate me specifically. His fiancée had died in an accident in the mountains two years before. He blamed Search and Rescue for not saving her life. I was captain of the team at the time."

"You must have been hurt very badly," she said.

"I was. But the medical personnel and my fellow SAR members saved my life. They put me back together, but I'll always have these scars."

"Then each one is like a photograph," she said. "A reminder that you were strong enough to live." She moved over him, sliding her body onto his, covering his imperfections with her perfection. He closed his eyes and welcomed her kisses, tracing his hands and his mouth over her with growing excitement.

He was kissing his way across her stomach when sense returned, and he stilled. He looked up at her.

"What's wrong?" she asked, and brushed his hair out of his eyes.

"I don't have a condom," he said. "I haven't been, um, sexually active in a while."

"Neither have I." She smiled. "It's okay. I'm on birth control. For other reasons. I think it's safe to say we're both healthy."

He slid up to kiss her on the lips again, then she was shifting beneath him, opening to him, urging him inside her. She wasn't shy about telling him what she wanted, and he was happy to comply. And when she began to move beneath him, he had no trouble following her lead. He slipped one hand beneath her hips to bring her closer and caressed her with the other until she was panting and moaning, and he knew any moment he would be gone.

She tensed around him, arching, and her release reverberated through him, triggering his own climax. He cried out. He might have said her name. He was past sensible thought, reacting with old instincts when he pulled her close and buried his face against her neck, chest heaving. She wiggled out from under him; he moved over to make room for her, and she lay, one thigh draped across his, curled against his side. "Was it worth the risk?" she whispered.

Still dazed, it took him a moment to realize what she was referring to. He hugged her closer. "Yes," he said, and closed his eyes.

THEY MADE LOVE again in the early morning, the first rays of sunlight streaming through the bedroom's one window, and Kelsey discovered a playful side to Tony. "I'm beginning to wonder about your fascination with my scars," he said as she kissed her way along the path a surgeon's scalpel had made to repair his injured left femur.

"Maybe I've always had fantasies about being with a bionic man," she said.

"There's one part of me that's never been injured and is one hundred percent original," he said, and pulled her up his body, his erection thrust against her.

"Are you sure you're ready to go again, old man?" she teased.

He let out a whoop and flipped her over on her back. "I'll show you *old*," he said, grinning, then proceeded to prove his vitality, much to her satisfaction.

The sun was up by the time they were both sated, the sheets a tangle. "Do you think Chris heard that?" she asked, then giggled.

"From what I've seen, he could sleep through an earthquake." Tony kissed her shoulder. "I'm going to make some coffee," he said, unwrapping himself from the covers and heading for the kitchen, giving her a lovely view of his naked backside and the corded muscles of his back. There wasn't an ounce of fat on the man, which was a little intimidating—and pretty impressive, too, despite his protestations that he wasn't handsome.

"I'm going to take a shower!" she called after him, half hoping he would join her.

When she emerged from the bathroom some ten minutes later, she found her way to the kitchen, where Chris grinned up at her from the kitchen table. "Good morning," he said around a mouthful of cold cereal. He finished chewing and wiped his mouth. "I saw the rag on the doorknob and figured we had company, so I made sure to get dressed before I wandered in here."

She laughed, even as her cheeks heated. She turned to pour a cup of coffee. "Where's Tony?"

"He got a call and went to take it outside." He turned back to his cereal.

She took her coffee to the table and sat across from him. "Are you always up this early?" she asked. Tony had said he usually came home late.

"Nope." He pushed the empty cereal bowl away. "But I have to be somewhere this morning. If it pans out, I might have to change my night owl ways."

"Oh?" She arched one eyebrow in question, but he merely shook his head.

"Can't tell you," he said. He glanced over his shoulder. "I especially can't tell Tony. Not yet."

Before she could question him further, he waved and left the room. Moments later, the motorcycle roared to life. Tony came through the back door. "Where's Chris off to so early?" he asked. "Did he say?"

She shook her head. She was surprised to find him already dressed in black tactical pants and a long-sleeved Eagle Mountain Search and Rescue tee. He held up his phone. "I got a call from Search and Rescue," he said. "A hiker is injured up on Kestrel Trail."

"The trail where you found Liz," she said. Just the name of the place made her heart beat faster.

He nodded. "It doesn't sound serious, but I need to go. We're shorthanded, with some of our most reliable volunteers out of town. I'll drop you by the inn on the way to SAR headquarters."

"Of course." She hurried to gather her purse and shoes, conscious that someone's life depended on her haste. She was shaking with nerves by the time they hustled to the car. "Are you really as calm as you look?" she asked as she buckled her seat belt.

"I'm going over in my mind everything we need to get together and what we'll have to do when we get there," he said. He glanced at her. "I'm not in good-enough shape yet to do much climbing, so I'll probably assist up top with rigging the ropes or wherever I'm needed."

"Is that hard, letting other people do what you've done before?" she asked.

"This work isn't about ego," he said. "It's about protecting each other and the patient."

He pulled in front of the Alpiner a few minutes later, and she opened the door. "Call me when you get back so I'll know you're safe," she said.

He leaned over and kissed her, a hard press of her lips to his. "Go," he said, and she went.

He was out of sight by the time she reached the front door. Hannah exited before she came in. "Was that Tony?" she asked.

Kelsey nodded. She hadn't planned on keeping her relationship with Tony secret, but arriving at the Alpiner with him at this time of morning was tantamount to an announcement that they had spent the night together.

To Hannah's credit, she didn't comment. "If I had known, I would have asked him for a ride," she said. "But Jake is coming to get me."

Kelsey went inside and up to her room. She lay on the bed, exhausted by the flood of emotion from these past days and hours. Could she do this? Could she be with a man who left at a moment's notice to put his life on the line? This was who Tony was, and she couldn't ask him to give it up. But could she really be that strong?

THE WORST SEARCH and rescue calls, the ones that stuck in people's memories and got written up in the paper, involved dangerous ascents of mountains, treacherous drops into canyons, treks over rough terrain in snow or fording icy rivers. Volunteers flirted with death as they battled the elements—and sometimes the injured persons themselves—to bring everyone to safety.

Then there were the calls like the one Eagle Mountain Search and Rescue responded to Wednesday morning. Good weather. A relatively minor injury on a marked trail. To the hiker who had slipped on loose rock and broken an ankle, the arrival of rescue volunteers was probably just as memorable as those other, more risky missions. But to Tony, Danny, Anna and Eldon, this save was a chance to be out in beautiful weather and lend a helping hand.

Carla Simmons was a fifty-five-year-old mother of three from Sacramento who had the bad luck to land the wrong way when she fell while hiking Kestrel Trail, ending up with a simple fracture of her right ankle. "You win a free ride down the mountain," Danny announced after examining her.

She looked up at them, pale and growing foggy-eyed from the pain medication Danny had administered. "Thank you," she said. "I'm sorry to be so much trouble."

"No trouble," Tony said. "It's a beautiful day to be on the mountain."

"I thought so, too, until I fell," she said.

They made quick work of splinting the fracture and making Carla as comfortable as possible on the litter. They were strapping her in for the trip down the trail when a voice hailed them. Tony looked up and was startled to see Ted striding toward them.

"What are you doing here, old man?" Danny asked.

"I was hiking and heard the call go out," Ted said. "Since I was nearby, I thought I'd see if you needed any help."

"We've got it all covered, thanks," Tony said.

Ted nodded and moved on. Tony turned back to their patient. "Funny coincidence, him being out here this morning," Danny said. Like Tony, he had been a member of SAR long enough to know Ted well.

"I think he gets bored sometimes," Tony said. "He misses SAR. It was such a big part of his life for so long." He thought sometimes about how he would cope if he had to leave the group.

Danny looked up the trail, in the direction Ted had walked. "Go get him and tell him he can give us a hand with this litter. He could probably use the exercise, and I trust him not to slack off."

Tony jogged up the trail. He hadn't gone far before he spotted Ted, off to the side, on the rocky bench where Liz's body had lain. "I keep thinking about that girl," Ted said as Tony approached.

Tony stepped up beside him. "Yeah. I find

myself on a rescue sometimes, and I'll remember another mission at that same place. You would think they would all blur together after a while—but for me, they don't."

"They don't for me, either," Ted said. "I keep wondering if there's something—some evidence—up here the cops didn't find." Ted kicked at the rock at their feet. "They were a bunch of bozos back then. None of them had any training in investigation. It's a wonder people didn't get away with murder every day."

"Sometimes law enforcement is able to solve cases a long time after the crime was committed," Tony said. "But I don't think it happens all that often."

"That girl, Kelsey, came to see me Sunday morning before the meeting," Ted said. "She thinks she's going to solve this thing, you know?"

"I know."

"She said the sheriff has DNA evidence and all she has to do is find a suspect for him to test. I told her if it was that easy, the cops would have done it a long time ago, but you know how kids are. They think they can do anything."

"Twenty-eight isn't exactly a *kid*," Tony said.

Ted grunted.

"Come on," Tony said. "We need you to help with this litter."

Ted straightened. "You do, do you?"

"We couldn't do it without you."

Ted nodded. "Then let's get to it." He set out ahead of Tony down the trail, back straight, head up. Looking younger than his sixty-two years.

Chapter Fourteen

Kelsey called the sheriff's department Wednesday afternoon. "I need an appointment with the sheriff," she said when Adelaide answered the phone. "I want to share with him everything I've found out about Liz's last days and ask him some questions."

She braced herself for a lecture about how the sheriff was a busy man, but all Adelaide said was, "He's here now, and I think this would be a good time if you can come on over."

Fifteen minutes later, she was seated across from the handsome sheriff, though Travis Walker looked a bit less pressed and polished than he had during their previous interview. His tie was loosened and his hair was a little mussed. He was staring at something in his hand when she entered the office, a look of deep concern on his face.

She waited for him to say something, but when he continued to stare at the square of paper in his hand, she cleared her throat. "Sheriff?" she asked.

He looked up and blinked, then straightened. "Hello, Ms. Chapman," he said. "I'm sorry, I'm a little distracted." He held out the piece of paper. "I just came from an ultrasound appointment with my wife. We're having twins, and they're due in six weeks. It's starting to seem very real."

His look of helplessness was so endearing she couldn't help but smile. "Congratulations," she said, and admired the image of two tiny infants curled around each other in their mother's womb. "That's a lot to take in, isn't it?" she asked.

He nodded, then opened the desk drawer and slid the photo inside. He smoothed his hand through his hair, then straightened his tie. When he addressed her again, he was all business. "Adelaide said you had some information about your sister?"

"I spoke with a former classmate of hers, Ben Everett," she said. "He lives in Junction now. He told me he asked Liz to be his date for the senior prom, but she turned him down. She said it was because she had an older boyfriend who was very jealous."

"Ben was interviewed at the time of Liz's

death, and there's nothing about that in the case file."

"He didn't say anything because he had promised Liz he wouldn't. He thought he was being honorable."

Travis took a stack of files from the corner of his desk. As he opened the top one, she recognized notes from the murder investigation. "Did he know who this older boyfriend was?" he asked.

"No. He tried to find out. He even followed Liz from school one day. But she saw him and ordered him to leave her alone."

"Do you think he's telling the truth?"

"I do. He said deputies interviewed him after Liz's body was found, and they accused him of killing her. He was frightened, and I believe if he had known anything that would throw suspicion on someone else, he would have done so."

Travis nodded and flipped through the pages in the file. "Have you learned anything else?"

She consulted the notes she had compiled from her interviews. "Some classmates of Liz's remember one night at the ice-cream parlor. She said she had to leave soon, that she was meeting someone. She wouldn't tell them who, and after she left, no one saw who she met."

"No one?" Travis asked. "Weren't they curious?"

"They say they didn't see anyone. But Veronica Olivares remembered that Ted Carruthers was standing on the sidewalk outside of a bar near the ice-cream parlor when Liz left. They thought he might have seen something. I asked him, but he says he doesn't remember. He didn't know Liz, and he had probably just stepped out to smoke a cigarette."

Travis nodded. "Anything else?"

"Nothing that you don't already know," she said. "Were there any suspects other than Ben and Tony? Were there any older men in town that they considered as her boyfriend?"

"I was in middle school when your sister was killed," he said. "I remember that it was a popular topic of conversation around town, and people were shocked when her body was discovered. But everything I know about the investigation is in these files." He tapped the stack of folders in front of him. "The same ones you saw."

"What about Mel Wheeler?" she asked.

Travis frowned. "Who is Mel Wheeler?"

"I was reviewing my notes this morning and came across his name," she said. "He was one of the Search and Rescue volunteers who helped retrieve Liz's body. He moved to Phoenix the year after her death."

"And you think he had something to do with your sister's murder?"

She flushed. "Probably not, but he was a man living in town at the time—so shouldn't you check him out?"

Travis grabbed a pen and made some notes on a yellow legal pad. "I'll see what I can find out."

She nodded. "Is there anyone in town who was on the force then?" she asked.

"No." The fine lines at the corners of his eyes tightened. "Some of them are in jail, and others moved away. The department started over with a clean slate."

"I feel like we're so close to figuring out the identity of Mountain Man," she said. "I can't believe, in a town this small, that someone didn't see Liz with him. She was the type of woman other people noticed."

"I heard someone attempted to run down you and Tony Meisner Monday night," he said.

The fact that he knew this jolted her. "Who told you that?" she asked.

"Tony mentioned it to Jake Gwynn. Tell me what happened."

"A car or truck ran up on the sidewalk and might have hit us both if we hadn't dived out of the way," she said.

"Did you see the car or driver?" the sheriff asked.

"No. The headlights were too bright. Tony said he thought it was a truck, though."

"Have you had any other threats? Anyone behaving suspiciously?"

"No. If that was someone who was upset about me digging into Liz's death, they've kept quiet since."

Travis closed the file. "If anything else happens that feels threatening, let us know. I can't stop you from talking to people about your sister, but consider that you could be endangering yourself."

"I'll be careful," she said, and stood to leave. She wasn't going to stop trying to find out information. Not when she felt she was so close to finding Liz's killer.

THE CALLOUT TO Kestrel Trail meant Tony reported late for work Wednesday, which meant getting off late also. When he finally got back to the house, he was surprised—but not displeased—to find Kelsey's car parked there. He went inside and followed the sound of voices to the back deck. She sat in a plastic chair across from the grill, where Chris was turning burgers.

"Hey, you're just in time for the party," Chris said. "The food's almost ready." He waved a spatula in the direction of a cooler next to Kelsey's chair. "Help yourself to a beer."

She planted her hand on the top of the cooler as he approached. "You have to pay the toll," she said.

"And what's the toll?"

"A kiss."

Aware of Chris's laughter behind him, he leaned in and gave her a kiss—a good, long one that had Chris making gagging noises.

They broke apart, laughing. Tony helped himself to a beer and settled into the chair next to Kelsey's. "Is there some special occasion?" he asked. "Or did you just feel like cooking?"

"Aren't you going to ask me why I'm not at Mo's, working?" Chris asked.

Tony frowned. "This isn't your night off?"

"I'm not at Mo's because I quit," Chris said.

Tony gripped his beer bottle tighter but forced himself not to shout. "Did something happen?" he asked.

Chris, spatula held aloft like a scepter, turned to face him once more. "Something happened," he said. "I got a new job."

Beside him, Kelsey's grin matched Chris's. The two of them were watching him, gleeful. Tony took a long sip of beer before he responded. "Where's the new job?"

"Eagle Surveying," Chris said. "I blew them away in my interview this morning, and they hired me on the spot."

Tony set his beer down carefully to avoid spilling it. "Eagle Surveying is where I work," he said carefully.

Chris's grin broadened. "Isn't it great?" He dragged over a chair and plopped down in front of them. "I'm going to be kind of a general gofer to start, but I'm thinking this fall, I can enroll in some online courses to work toward my degree and eventually get my license."

"What made you decide on surveying?" he asked.

"I passed you one day out on the highway," Chris said. "You were out there in the woods on a beautiful day, just you and one other guy in a truck—no office, no one looking over your shoulder. I did a little research into it, and it sounded like something I would like."

"It's not all beautiful days and being on your own," Tony said. "Some days you're out in pouring rain or broiling heat. And you still have bosses and customers to answer to."

"Yeah, yeah, I know all that," Chris said. "But I still think this is the career for me. I start tomorrow. Some guy named Curtis is going to train me, but it probably won't be long before I'm working with you." He stood. "Who's ready for burgers?"

Kelsey leaned toward Tony. "He's so excited about this," she said. "He wants to be just like you."

Tony snorted and picked up his beer. "I don't know why he'd want that."

"He really does look up to you," she said. She leaned closer still and whispered, "Tell him you're proud of him."

He didn't say anything.

She sat back. "I'm sorry," she said. "It really isn't any of my business."

"No." He took her hand. "I'm glad you care so much. We just don't talk about that kind of stuff."

She patted his hand. "Then maybe you should."

"Here you go." Chris handed them plates full of burgers and potato chips.

"Thanks." Tony accepted the plate, then raised his beer. "To another surveyor in the family."

"To Chris," Kelsey said, and they clinked bottles while Chris beamed.

Tony had a flash of memory, of a seven-year-old Chris astride a new bike, on one of Tony's infrequent visits. "Watch me, Uncle Tony!" he called, and popped a wheelie in the family driveway.

"Way to go!" Tony shouted and pumped his fist, and Chris had pumped his own fist in imitation and sped away, shouting at the top of his lungs, "Way to goooooo!"

They had both come so far in that time…but maybe not that far after all.

ON KELSEY'S SECOND morning of returning to the Alpiner at dawn in Tony's truck, she was greeted at the door by Brit Richards, Hannah's mother. "Good morning," Brit said cheerily. "Aren't you the early bird."

Kelsey tried to fake looking like someone who had risen early and not been out all night, but she realized she wasn't fooling anyone when Brit said, "Next time, invite Tony in for a cup of coffee. We always enjoy seeing him."

Kelsey nodded and scurried up to her room, vowing to herself that next time, she would insist on going back to the Alpiner to spend the night, no matter how hard it was to leave Tony's bed. Between Chris's smirks and teasing over the breakfast table and Brit's knowing looks, she felt too many people were far too interested in what went on in Tony's bedroom. Better to let them guess.

After a nap and a shower, Kelsey left the inn to walk around town. She tried to think of someone else to talk to or someplace to go. Maybe she should find out the address of the place Liz had listed as her residence and visit there. Deborah Raymond had told her Liz had never lived there, but maybe she had lived nearby. Kelsey might see a neighboring house or apartment and realize it was exactly the kind of place Liz would have liked.

But that was a fantasy. Wherever Liz had lived, Mountain Man had been there, and Kelsey had no idea what her sister's mysterious suitor had been like. Instead, she walked through a neighborhood two blocks off Main and tried to imagine Liz here, in her low-cut jeans and cropped shirt, strolling these same streets, exploring her new home.

She had walked about a block when she suddenly had the sensation of being watched. Goose bumps prickled on her arms, and she whipped around, trying to spot whoever was spying on her. But she saw no one. She kept walking, faster now, turning her head from side to side to try to see who might be looking at her. Was someone really watching, or was she imagining this sensation?

"Hey, Kelsey!"

Tammy Patterson hailed Kelsey from across the street, then hurried to catch up with her. "I'm glad I ran into you," Tammy said. "I was going to call and tell you the story is going to run in the next issue—unless some big news pushes it out, but things like that seldom happen around here. So look for it Tuesday."

"Thanks so much for writing the story," Kelsey said.

"I hope it helps you find out more about what happened to your sister." Tammy squeezed her arm and hurried away.

Kelsey turned to head back toward the inn and almost collided with Ted Carruthers. "Whoa, there!" he said, steadying her. He looked past her. "Is that reporter bugging you?"

"No." She stepped back, out of his grasp. "She's great. Tammy wrote an article about my search for my sister's killer."

Ted frowned, bushy white eyebrows drawing together. "You really think that's a good idea?" he asked.

"Why wouldn't it be a good idea?"

"You might upset the wrong person."

"I hope I *do* upset the man who killed Liz."

"How do you know it was a man?"

"Fine. The *person* who killed Liz. I hope they read that article and know they aren't going to get away with murder."

"Finding out who killed her isn't going to bring your sister back," he said.

The comment enraged her. "I know that." What did he know about Liz or her family's grief? "The person who killed Liz deserves to pay for what he did," she said. "And yes, I think it was probably a man—the man she moved to

Eagle Mountain to be with. He doesn't deserve to walk around free when she'll never have that chance again." Her voice broke on the words, and she turned and fled, not wanting to deal with him anymore. Not wanting him to see how much she felt the loss of a sister she hadn't spoken to in twenty years. Nothing she could do would bring Liz back, but her sister would always be part of her. The killer would never be able to take that away.

TONY AND CHRIS fell into the habit of having breakfast together in the morning, then leaving for work—Chris on his motorcycle to shadow Curtis Lefsen, who was training him on his duties as a surveyor's assistant; and Tony in his truck, to either the job site or the office to pick up Brad or another assistant. Often, Chris got home earlier than Tony and had dinner ready by the time Tony came in. Over spaghetti or tacos or whatever Chris had made, they would talk about work and Chris's plans to study for his surveyor's license. "I always liked math in school," Chris said during one of these conversations. "This is putting all those abstract principles in algebra and trigonometry and stuff to work in the real world."

"I thought you didn't like school," Tony said.

He remembered Eddie complaining that his youngest never applied himself.

"I hated school," Chris said. "But that's because teachers made the classes so boring. Surveying is really interesting."

"I'm pretty sure to get your degree, you have to take English and history and everything else," Tony said.

Chris shrugged. "I can do it. I never had trouble learning stuff. I just didn't see the point. Now I do."

Tony did the dishes while Chris texted with friends or watched TV. He had thought having someone else in the house all the time, making noise and moving things around, would annoy him, but now he missed his nephew when he was out with friends. No more young women had appeared on the couch, though Chris had mentioned going out with Amy again. Maybe they had found somewhere else for their assignations.

He was musing over this on the Wednesday after Chris had started work at Eagle Surveying when his text alert sounded. His first thought was that it was Kelsey, letting him know she was on the way over. She had gotten into the habit of coming over after dinner most nights. She had extended her stay at the Alpiner and hadn't said anything about when she might leave town. Tony wasn't going to ask.

But the text was from Sheri: Injured skier on Mount Baker, Raven Couloir. Report to HQ ASAP.

Tony dropped the dish towel and headed toward his bedroom to change. "I got a call and have to go out," he said as he passed through the living room.

Chris looked up from the television. "Someone's hurt?"

Tony didn't answer, but Chris followed him into his bedroom. "Who's hurt?" Chris asked.

"A skier. On Mount Baker."

"What was he doing up there?" Chris asked.

"Probably skiing down." Tony shucked off his sweatpants and pulled on a pair of insulated climbing pants. It would be cold up on the mountain at night. "This time of year, you can climb up and ski down in one day." He had done it himself several years before. The trip had been exhilarating, especially the final descent through the snow-filled couloir, the kind of expedition that tested every skill and made a person feel that much more accomplished and alive.

"Is there anything I can do to help?" Chris asked.

"You can finish the dishes," Tony said. He pulled on a thermal layer, then a heavy fleece.

"When will you be back?"

"When the job is done." He grabbed his parka, his radio and his keys and headed toward the door. His pack and climbing gear were already in the truck. The familiar adrenaline surged through him, making him move faster and think more clearly. Someone needed him and he was ready.

CHRIS ANSWERED KELSEY'S knock on Tony's door. He stared at her, a confused look on his face. "Hey, Kelsey," he said after a bit. "Um, Tony's not here."

She glanced over her shoulder and realized Tony's truck wasn't in the driveway. "Where is he?" she asked.

"He got a call out from Search and Rescue. Something about an injured skier on Mount Baker. He didn't call you?"

"I haven't talked to him since early this morning." They had talked then about her coming over after supper to hang out.

"He was probably too focused on the call." Chris held the door open wider. "You want to come in and wait with me?"

She started to say no, she'd go back to the hotel, but changed her mind when she saw the pleading look in Chris's eyes. "Sure," she said, moving past him. "It will be good to have company."

"I don't know why I'm freaked out," Chris said. "Tony does this stuff all the time. I guess this is the first time it really hit me how dangerous it is. I don't like thinking about him on some mountain in the dark."

Kelsey shivered. She had thought about search and rescue work only in terms of the end results—people found or saved, their injuries tended. She had avoided contemplating the danger to the rescuers themselves. "I'm sure he'll be okay," she said. "Tony has done this lots of times."

"You know he was hurt really badly last year, don't you?" Chris said.

She settled onto the sofa. "But he's better now."

"He likes people to think so, but you haven't seen him. By the end of some days, he's in so much pain he can hardly move. I hear him up at night, pacing around."

She shook her head. "He's always fine when he's with me."

"He doesn't want you to know. He doesn't want anyone to know. But I figure it takes a lot longer than a year to recover from something like that."

"I'm sure he'll be fine," she said, and hugged a pillow to her stomach. And when he was back, she'd ask a few more questions. Was he really in pain every day? She would make it clear he didn't have to hide something like that from her.

Chris's smile struck her as forced. "So, how are things with you?" he asked. "How's the sleuthing going?"

"I keep running into dead ends," she admitted. "I heard from the sheriff today about a man I'd asked him to check out, and he probably wasn't the killer."

"Who was that?" Chris asked.

"Mel Wheeler. He was with Search and Rescue, part of the team that retrieved Liz's body from Kestrel Trail. He moved to Phoenix a year after Liz died, but Sheriff Walker was able to track him down. Or rather, he tracked down Mel's widow. She says she and Mel were vacationing in Cancun around the time Liz disappeared, and she sent him pictures to prove it. It was her birthday, and the hotel presented her with a cake with the date written on it." She blew out a breath. "It was a long shot anyway."

"I'm glad it wasn't him," Chris said. "I mean, that would be freaky, wouldn't it—someone who went out of his way to help strangers turning out to be a killer?"

"I don't know," she mused. "Isn't it almost a

cliché for a murderer's neighbors and friends to talk about what a nice guy he was? And Liz obviously trusted him enough to leave her family to be with him. There had to have been a good side to him for that to happen."

"He had a twisted view of love if he ended up killing her," Chris said.

"He did." Love was complicated for everyone to navigate, but at least most people didn't have to worry about the person they loved killing them.

That is, if her sister's killer really was Mountain Man. What if she was on the wrong track and a random hiker she'd met on the trail murdered Liz? She had been so sure that hard work and a fresh look at the evidence would lead her to the right suspect—but she had to admit, if only to herself, that she might never find the right person. Whoever had killed Liz, he might never be punished. And Kelsey and her mom would never know what really happened all those years ago. The idea left a hollow feeling in the center of her chest. She had lived all these years without knowing, but it felt worse, somehow, to be here where Liz had lived, to talk to the people who knew her and know that she might leave with no more answers than when she had arrived, only more questions.

Chapter Fifteen

As was often the case in a small community, Tony knew the people involved in this callout. Nick Teague and Tyler Hanran had decided to take advantage of the good spring snow on Mount Baker to ski down the central couloir to a forest service road where they could leave a car for the drive back to town.

"Everything was going great," Tyler told the assembled volunteers at Search and Rescue headquarters. "Until about a third of the way down. We hadn't accounted for the warmer temperatures yesterday and all the sun that was hitting that face. The snow got really crusty and icy. Nick was ahead of me, feeling out the route. It looked like he was doing great and then he just...slid." Tyler spread his hands wide in a gesture of helplessness. "I thought he was going to be okay and self-correct, but his ski must have caught an edge or something, and he started to cartwheel." He wiped a hand across his face.

"It was terrible. I thought for sure he was dead. I stood there a long time, looking at him lying there, so still. Then I saw movement. I shouted down to him, and he kind of groaned. I was afraid if I tried to go down the same way he had, I would fall, too. And if I tried to climb down the rock directly above him, I could send a boulder down on him. So I moved way over to the left of him, took off my skis and climbed down this gnarly pitch to a point below him, then climbed up to him."

"Do you know exactly where he landed?" Captain Sheri Stevens asked.

"He's on this scree ledge about a third of the way into the col." Tyler pulled out his phone. "I've got GPS coordinates."

Tony imagined the collective sigh of relief from the assembled volunteers. For most of his time with Search and Rescue, finding someone on a mountain meant making an educated guess as to where they lay and relying on sharp vision and luck. Technology allowed them to zero in on the person needing help much more quickly and accurately.

"What's his condition?" Hannah asked.

Tyler grimaced. "He's pretty banged up. His left leg is facing backwards, and he was in a lot of pain. I was afraid to move him. Oh, and he's got two broken fingers and maybe broken ribs. He said it hurt a lot to breathe. I taped the fingers together and piled all the spare clothes we had in our packs on him. I gave him all our water, too. I hated to leave him, but I had to get help."

"It sounds like you did all the right things," Hannah said.

"How did you get down?" Tony asked. That might be a good route up to the patient.

"I inched my way along this narrow ledge to the summer hiking trail and hiked down," Tyler said. "It's really steep and icy, but I was so worried about Nick I just gutted it out."

"There's a lot of snow on the ledges above that trail," Ryan said. "With the warmer weather today, it's an avalanche risk."

"Jake, contact the avalanche center for a report," Sheri said. "And I need a weather report for tomorrow. We can't risk sending people up that trail in the dark."

"There's a full moon tonight," Tony said. "And the colder temperatures will mean more stable snow. Still a risk, but we could do it."

"Better for Nick than spending the night waiting," Carrie said.

Sheri considered this. "Night-climbing isn't my favorite thing, but I've done it."

"The moon on the snow can make it pretty

bright," Ryan said. "Almost as good as daylight."

"Then let's do it." Sheri moved to the map of the area pinned to the wall. "I want a team headed up the north side to the couloir," she said, indicating the route. "We'll send a south team up as far as it's deemed safe and see if there's another route they can take."

Tony, Sheri, Ryan and Caleb, a rookie volunteer who had skied the same route Nick and Tyler had taken only the week before, gathered around a map of Mount Baker to plot strategy while others assembled equipment. Lieutenant Carrie Andrews started making phone calls, trying to find a helicopter and flight crew that could lift Nick off the mountain.

Tony was part of the south-approach team, with Jake, Grace and Caleb. Sheri, Ryan, Eldon and Danny, the team's best mountaineers, made up the north team, which was expected to have the best chance of reaching the ledge in the couloir where Nick lay. Tyler wanted to go back up with them, but they persuaded him he was too exhausted and would only slow them down.

"I've got a chopper coming in from Durango at first light," Carrie reported. "But whether they can make the lift is at their discretion." As always, the flight crew had the final say as to whether the rescue was safe enough for them to attempt.

The teams were heading for the parking lot when Ted pulled up in his truck. "I heard the call was all hands on deck," he said. "What can I do?"

"Come with me," Carrie said. She was incident commander for this mission. "You can run resupply back and forth from town."

Tony volunteered to carry one of the oxygen canisters. "You're just a glutton for punishment, aren't you?" Jake said as he helped strap the heavy canister onto Tony's pack.

"If I get tired, I'll give it to you," Tony said. Jake might be younger, but he wasn't in the shape Tony was in, and he and Jake both knew it.

Ted joined them with two thermoses of coffee. "You'll appreciate these when you get up there," he said. He handed one to Jake and tucked the other into Tony's pack. "Heard anything from Kelsey lately?" he asked.

"Kelsey is fine," Tony said. Why was Ted asking about Kelsey now?

"I thought maybe she had left town by now."

"Not yet," Tony said. She would probably leave soon. He was trying to accept that while also not thinking about it.

They headed out and, twenty minutes later,

started up the trail. The first mile was almost pleasant, the snow having receded to reveal a dry, packed trail. The moon was bright enough they didn't need their headlamps. But as soon as they hit the tree line, the conditions began to deteriorate—patches of frozen mud and loose rock, then slippery ice. The mud built up in the treads of their hiking boots, which made finding purchase on the ice difficult. They continually had to stop to scrape their boots on rocks. They tried jogging up the trail, but that proved almost impossible.

By the time they reached the exposed west-facing section of the trail, they were already flagging, and Tony's repaired legs and shoulder throbbed with every step. He thought about handing the oxygen canister off to Jake but fought against the idea.

They paused at a small bench that gave them a good view of the slopes above—rocky ridges frosted with heavy snow like dollops of frosting on a cake. Tony radioed to Carrie. "This place looks like an avalanche waiting to happen," he said.

"Can you cut over up the gulley to the west?" she asked. "Caleb says there's a ledge there that's protected and will take you across most of the way to the spot where Nick is."

"Ten-four," Tony said. "We'll head that way."

The cut-across was slow going. They all wanted to rush but knew they couldn't. Endangering themselves and the others with them wouldn't help save Nick. They had just reached the ledge when the radio crackled again. "Stand down," Carrie said. "Sheri and her team have reached Nick. We need you all back down here to ferry supplies to them."

So they turned around and went back down. The descent was faster, though they slid more than once in the slick mud. Back at the trailhead, they jogged over to Grace's Subaru, stored their gear and raced to the north staging area, where Carrie sent them up that route laden with the oxygen canister, food and another set of radios for talking with the helicopter pilots.

Though they all would have liked to stay to see the rest of the rescue, the avalanche danger was too high to risk it, so they left Nick with Danny and Ryan. Pale golden light was showing over the mountains by the time they reached the staging area once more, where they listened to the distant bass throb of the Chinook helicopter arriving, twin rotors cutting through the air with a sound like a heartbeat.

Tony, Carrie and Jake climbed a hundred feet up the trail to a ledge that gave them a view of the helicopter hovering above the couloir. They passed a pair of binoculars back and forth and watched as a long line with what looked like a hook on the end lowered toward the snow field. Moments later, the line retreated back toward the belly of the aircraft, a bundle that resembled a burrito swinging beneath it. They all cheered when the litter was safely pulled into the chopper. Nick Teague was safe.

Then the tension wound tight again as the hook descended a second time, much faster. It ascended faster, too, but Tony could just make out two figures clinging to it. They were almost to the belly of the chopper when the snow field gave way, a wave of white rippling down the couloir, powder billowing into the air like steam. The line jerked into the chopper, and it rose up with another jerk and swept away.

Sheri keyed the radio. "Ryan, what's your status?"

"Everyone is okay," he radioed back. "Nick is stable. Danny is monitoring him."

"We saw the avalanche," Sheri said.

"Yeah. We got out of there just in time."

KELSEY WOKE, groggy and with a stiff neck. She had fallen asleep on the sofa. Chris was slumped in the chair across from her, head back, snoring softly. She grabbed her phone from the coffee table and stared at the digital display. 5:35 a.m. And Tony still wasn't back?

She was trying to decide whom she might call to find out if he was all right when the phone buzzed in her hand. She answered the unfamiliar number, and Brit Richards's cheery voice greeted her. "Kelsey, we're getting ready to take some food to Search and Rescue headquarters," Brit said. "Do you want to come with us?"

"Are they back?" Kelsey asked. "Is everyone okay?"

"I just spoke to Hannah, and she said the rescue went well," Brit said. "Everyone safe and sound, including the young man they were sent to help. But everyone is going to be exhausted and hungry. Thad and I are picking up food from Mo's to take to them."

"Of course I'll help." She looked across at Chris, who had sat up and was rubbing his face with his hands. "Chris and I will both help."

"Then hurry and meet us at Mo's."

Kelsey pocketed her phone and stood. "Come on," she told Chris. "We have to get to Mo's and help take food to Search and Rescue headquarters."

"They're back?" He looked around. "What time is it?"

"After five thirty. Come on. Brit is waiting."

At Mo's, she and Chris loaded into the car with Thad and Brit and what looked like three dozen to-go boxes of pizza, wings and nachos.

The parking lot at Search and Rescue headquarters was filled with cars. "It looks like a party," Kelsey said as she helped unload the food.

"It is," Brit said. "Some of these people are family of the volunteers, and some of them are just neighbors who want to congratulate them or hear about the mission."

They trooped into the building, boxes piled up to their noses, and were relieved of their burden as soon as they entered. "Food!" someone bellowed, and a crowd of men and women surged forward. Kelsey spotted Tony with a slice of pizza in one hand and a chicken wing in the other and worked her way through the scrum toward him.

"Kelsey!" He popped the last of the pizza into his mouth, then pulled her close in a hug. "I'm sorry I couldn't see you last night, but Chris told you what was going on, right?"

"He did." She slapped his chest. "I was a little worried about you, though."

"Oh, I'm fine." He hugged her tighter. "Let's sit down." He pulled her to the end of a long table and gingerly lowered himself into a folding chair. Someone slid a pizza box toward him, and he snagged another slice. "Do you want something to eat?" he asked between mouthfuls.

She shook her head. "Are you okay?"

"I'm fine." He grimaced. "Sore. Stiff. Tired.

And starving. But that's normal after a mission."

He looked good—sun-burnt and wind-blown but elated. "I take it the rescue went well?"

He nodded. "Everybody worked together to pull it off. Exactly like it's supposed to work."

Chris set a box of wings on the table in front of them. "How's it going?" he asked.

"I'm okay." Tony grabbed his hand. "Thanks for coming out." He looked around them. "Do you all know my nephew, Chris?" He introduced the young man to the volunteers around them. Kelsey heard the pride in his voice, and Chris was smiling so widely his face probably hurt.

Cheers rose from the crowd as two men moved through the crowd. They settled into chairs across from Tony and Kelsey and were immediately handed plates piled high with pizza and wings. "This is Ryan and Tyler," Tony said, pointing to each. "This is Kelsey."

They nodded to her and continued eating. "How is Nick?" someone asked.

"His right leg is a mess, but the surgeons will put him back together," Danny said. "Fractured ribs, broken finger. He's lucky Tyler was with him and got to us as soon as he could."

"If that slab had fractured while he was lying

there in the couloir, he'd have been wiped out," Ryan said.

"I heard you got a free ride in a helicopter." A blonde with green eyes slipped in behind Ryan and wrapped her arms around him.

He smiled up at her. "Riding that hook up might have been a kick if I'd had time to enjoy it," he said.

"The pilot was yelling at us to hurry, hurry, he could see the snow started to fracture," Danny said. "I barely had time to grab hold before he starting hauling the line up. I almost wet my pants I was so terrified."

"Then I'm really glad you were hanging on below me," Ryan said.

The others laughed, and Danny reached for another slice of pizza. Tony slid his arm around Kelsey. "I was almost as happy to see you as I was to see this food," he said.

"'Almost'?"

He took a bite of pizza. "I must have hiked ten miles today with a heavy pack," he said. "I was starving."

"You get used to it," the blonde with Ryan addressed Kelsey. She held out her hand. "I'm Deni Traynor, by the way."

"Sorry." Tony set aside his slice of pizza. "Deni, this is Kelsey Chapman. Deni is Ryan's fiancée."

"Nice to meet you." Deni ruffled Ryan's hair. "He'll come home and sleep for twenty hours, get up and eat half the refrigerator, then be fine until the next hard call." She kissed his cheek. "My hero."

Ryan grimaced. "You know I hate that. It's a team effort. Nobody is a hero. Everybody is just working together to do a good job."

Danny and Tony murmured agreement. Ryan's girlfriend sent Kelsey a knowing look.

When Kelsey looked away, she found Tony watching her. She leaned closer. "It's like a big family, isn't it?" she said. Because she was with Tony, everyone around him accepted her. She had never experienced anything like it.

He squeezed her knee under the table. "I guess it can be a little overwhelming."

She shook her head. "No. It's really nice."

Ted carried a chair over to their table. "Move over," he said, and nudged Danny's shoulder.

Danny pushed his chair back. "I'm going to go find Carrie," he said before he left.

Ted set his chair against the wall and took the seat vacated by Danny. "Hello, Kelsey," he said.

"Hello, Ted."

"How's your detective work going?" he asked. "Have you found your suspect?"

"No."

"I've been thinking a lot about this," Ted

said. "There was a guy in town back then—Ray somebody or other. He worked as a janitor at the high school, then they found out he'd been charged with rape back in Colorado Springs but let go on a technicality. He would have known your sister since he worked at the high school. Did the sheriff's department ever take a look at him?"

"Ray Jackman," Kelsey said. "The sheriff questioned him. But he was out of town during the time Liz would have been killed, at a hearing back in Colorado Springs. And his DNA wasn't a match."

"Well, who's to say that DNA was even from the killer?" Ted said. "It could have been from anyone."

"I don't think Liz would have fought with anyone else that day," Tony said.

"Why didn't the cops just look for a guy with a scratched-up face?" Ted asked. "I don't remember anyone like that at the time."

"I don't know." Kelsey was aware of everyone around them watching her. She had been feeling so good, and Ted had spoiled the mood. "I don't want to talk about that now," she said. "I want to hear more about what happened last night."

They began talking about the rescue again, and she settled back against Tony. He had stopped eating and laced his hand with hers.

She didn't understand half of what the rescuers were saying as they discussed the technical aspects of the mission, but it didn't matter. She let the words wash over her, the tension of the night giving way to a contentment she didn't think she had ever known before.

KELSEY RETURNED TO the Alpiner with Brit and Thad later that morning. As much as she would have liked to stay with Tony, she could see he was exhausted and in pain. He didn't protest when she suggested he go home and recover, and his parting kiss was as warm as ever.

Back at the inn, she called her mother. "Oh, hello, Kelsey." The volume of the television in the background lowered. "Are you home yet?"

"I'm still in Eagle Mountain," Kelsey said. "I'm still trying to find out what happened to Liz."

"Have you learned anything?" her mother asked.

"Not yet. But I'm still researching."

Canned laughter from the television. "If you haven't found out anything after all this time, I don't think you will," her mother said. "Maybe your father was right. We should forget all about this. None of it is going to bring Liz back. None of it is going to make things right."

What was *right* to her mother? Liz never having left? That was probably part of it. "Don't you want to know what happened?" Kelsey asked.

"I don't know any more what I want. We've lived all these years not knowing. I buried my daughter once. Why should I want to dig her up again? I've lived more of my life without Liz than with her. If she had stayed, maybe things would have been worse. She was always such a headstrong child. If she had lived, she might have still been a disappointment."

"Am I a disappointment?" Kelsey knew as soon as the words were out that she shouldn't have asked. There was no right answer to that. A long silence, so long she wondered if her mother had hung up. "Mom?"

"You couldn't be a disappointment to me," her mother said. "I never expected anything from you. With Liz gone, I didn't have it in me."

The truth, unvarnished and as painful as raw wood, full of splinters. "I'm thinking of staying in Eagle Mountain," Kelsey blurted out. She hadn't even considered this until now, but as soon as she said it, she realized it was what she wanted. Maybe what she needed.

Her mother sighed. "So you're going to abandon me, too."

You abandoned me a long time ago, Kelsey thought. *You and Dad both.* But she didn't say it. "I'd still visit and call," she said.

"You do what you want to do," her mother said. "It doesn't matter to me."

It ought to matter, Kelsey thought after she ended the call. But Liz ought to have lived. Her killer ought to have been caught. Life was full of things that ought to be and didn't happen.

Chapter Sixteen

The next morning Tony woke to stabbing pain in his legs and a deep ache in his arms and shoulders. For a moment of disorientation, he thought he was back in the hospital, shortly after the accident, and his recovery had been merely a dream. But after another moment, full awareness returned, along with the memory of the previous day's rescue.

He had hiked miles over rough terrain yesterday, lugging heavy equipment. He remembered hurting then, too, but the pain had been tempered by the adrenaline and the urgency of the mission. Today, even getting out of bed was agony. He struggled to get to the bathroom and stared into the mirror, at the dark circles under his eyes. He looked almost as bad as he felt.

He brushed his teeth with shaking hands, then found his phone and dialed the number for his doctor. "It's possible you reinjured something," the nurse practitioner said. "Let's get you in this morning and make sure."

He texted his boss that he wouldn't be in to work that day. Bruce would have heard about yesterday's rescue by now and was used to Tony coming in late or not at all after a particularly complicated mission. Tony always made up the work and rarely took time off for any other reason.

He sat on the edge of the bed for a long time, gathering strength for the task of getting dressed. After a while, Chris knocked on the door. "You okay in there?" he asked.

"I'm fine," Tony said. "I already talked to Bruce. I'm not going in today."

The door opened and Chris leaned in. "What's wrong?" he asked. "Did you get hurt on that rescue and didn't tell anyone?"

"I'm fine." He shifted on the side of the bed. "I'm just a little stiff. I'm going to the doctor to make sure everything is okay."

"I could stay home and drive you," Chris said. "Or get Kelsey to go with you."

"No!" He didn't want Kelsey to see him like this. He shoved to his feet, trying not to grimace as he did so. "Go on. I'll be fine."

When Chris had left, he sank onto the bed again. What had he done? All those months of rehab thrown out the window for what? Because he wanted to be a hero? Because he craved the rush of being so needed? He grimaced, knowing how close to the truth that really was.

His phone rang and he glanced at the screen. Kelsey. He groaned. He couldn't talk to her right now. He wouldn't be able to hide how terrible he felt, and he didn't want her to know him like this. She deserved better.

Who was he kidding? She was going to leave anyway. Her home was in Iowa—her family and friends, her job. This thing between them was never going to be permanent, and he needed to accept that.

He gritted his teeth and pulled on pants and a shirt, forced his feet into shoes, then grabbed his keys and hobbled to his truck. By the time he hauled himself into the driver's seat, he was sweating and gasping for air like an eighty-year-old. Ha! He knew eighty-year-olds who were in better shape than he was right now.

He shoved the key into the ignition and started the engine. Driving itself wasn't too bad. At the doctor's office, he managed to slide out of the driver's seat and walk gingerly into the orthopedic office.

An hour and a half and a series of X-rays and a painful physical examination later, his doctor announced—with far more cheer than Tony appreciated—that there was no permanent damage. "You just overdid it," the doctor said. "You have to remember you're not in the shape you used to be. You need to take it a little easier. Dial it back a notch."

Except Tony didn't know how to do anything but go at the work full-tilt.

He left with a prescription for more physical therapy, some heavy-duty anti-inflammatories and instructions to "take it a little easier."

He collapsed onto the sofa as soon as he made it home, the doctor's words on repeat in his head. If he took it easy, that meant other team members had to pick up the slack. That wasn't acceptable, at least not to him. He had told himself he could live with pain and discomfort—a little suffering was part of rescue work in all weather conditions on usually rough terrain. But he was used to bouncing back quickly. What did it mean that he was in such bad shape right now?

His phone rang again, and he pulled it out, only to see Kelsey's name. What would happen if he didn't answer? Would she keep calling, or would she be angry he blew her off? "Hello?" he answered.

"Hi, Tony. I'm not interrupting you, am I?"

"Not really."

"How are you doing after yesterday? You must be exhausted."

"I'm a little tired."

"Do you want me to bring dinner over? We could chill and watch TV or something."

"No. I think I'm going to make it an early night. Don't come over."

"Oh." Was he imagining the disappointment in that single syllable? "If you're sure?"

"I'm sure. And I have to go now." He ended the call before she could say more, then tossed the phone onto the coffee table and fell back on the sofa. Wanting to see Kelsey was an ache almost worse than the pain in his legs, but he couldn't let her see him like this. When she went back to Iowa, he didn't want this image of him, broken, to be the one she took with her.

KELSEY TRIED NOT to be hurt that Tony hadn't wanted to see her. Maybe he had a routine after a tough rescue like this and he didn't want her interfering with whatever it was. She should respect that and not react as if he was rejecting her. But believing this and actually controlling her emotions were two different things. He had been so abrupt on the phone, as if he couldn't wait to hang up on her. All the warmth and closeness they had developed had vanished. When he ended the call, it was like having a door slammed in her face.

She kept herself busy the rest of the day. She

went through her notes yet again and tried to watch TV, forcing herself not to contact Tony. But the fact that he didn't call her weighed on her and made sleep elusive.

When she came down for breakfast Friday morning, she was feeling grumpier than usual, though she tried to hide it when Hannah breezed into the breakfast room and headed for her table.

"Hey, Kelsey," Hannah said. She paused, one hand on the back of the empty chair at the table across from Kelsey.

"Hey, Hannah." Kelsey sat up straighter and forced a smile. "How are you this morning?"

"I'm good. I was just wondering if you've talked to Tony last night or this morning?"

"I talked to him for a little bit yesterday afternoon."

"Is he okay?"

"He said he was tired and was going to turn in early."

Hannah frowned. "I bet he overdid it on that rescue Wednesday," she said. "I could see he was in pain, though he was trying to hide it. Did he say if he had talked to his doctor?"

"He didn't mention that." They hadn't really had much of a conversation.

"I'm just worried because he didn't show up for the SAR meeting last night," Hannah said. "I've never known him to miss a meeting before."

"I was thinking I'd go over to his house and check on him this morning," Kelsey said. "See if he needs anything."

She had been thinking no such thing until this moment, but now she could hardly wait to get to him.

"That would be great," Hannah said. "Let me know if there's anything I can do."

Kelsey finished her coffee, then grabbed her car keys from the room and headed out toward Tony's house. If he was upset that she was coming over unannounced, she would make him understand it was because she cared about him. If he was hurting, she wanted to help.

She rang the bell, then waited a long time for him to answer. She couldn't hear anything inside the house, but Tony's truck sat in the driveway. She rang again. What if he had passed out or something? Or fallen and broken a bone? Could she break in and find him? She reached for the door to see if it was unlocked, just as the door swung open.

Tony stared down at her. "You look terrible!" she said, then covered her mouth, as if she could take back the words. But it was true—he was hunched and pale, his beard untrimmed, hair uncombed.

"You need to leave," he said, and tried to close the door, but she pushed past him.

"Hannah told me she thought you overdid it on that rescue, and it looks like she was right," she said. She moved to his side and took his arm. "Have you talked to your doctor?"

He pulled his arm away. "I'm all right. I just need some rest."

The sharpness of his words stung. Fair enough. He didn't like being fussed over, so how about a little tough love? "You can't blow me off the way you did yesterday and not expect me to worry," she said.

"You don't need to worry about me." He turned away, and she followed as he lurched back to the sofa. She surreptitiously looked for signs that he had been self-medicating with liquor or pills but saw no indications of that—just a water bottle and a half-eaten sandwich on the coffee table.

She sat next to the sandwich, facing him where he half sprawled on the sofa. "I know we haven't known each other very long," she said. "But I care about you. It hurts me to see you hurting."

A look of confusion passed through his eyes before he turned away. "You can't do anything about the pain."

"Maybe not the physical pain," she said. "But you must be hurting inside, too, if you're pushing me away." Was that too much? she wondered. Did she sound like an amateur psychologist, trying to diagnose him?

"I'm going to be fine," he grumbled.

She moved from the coffee table to the sofa and sat with her hip and thigh touching his. "Do you want to be miserable by yourself, or maybe a little less miserable with me here, too?"

He made a choking sound, and she wondered if he was sobbing, then he turned his head toward her, and she realized he was laughing. She smiled, and he pulled her to him. Then they were kissing, wild hungry kisses that made her heart race, a little out of control.

He pulled her onto his lap, and soon they were undressing each other, moving a little awkwardly to accommodate his legs, which apparently hurt him a great deal, and his shoulder, also tender. But she didn't mind. She liked sitting on top of him like this, urging him to lie back while she worked her way down his body, aware of him watching her with a hungry look. And when they came together, she watched passion ease some of the tension from his body and drain the anger from his eyes. When he reached out to caress her, she smiled and told herself everything would be all right. The two of them were too good together for this not to work.

SOMETIME DURING THE NIGHT, they did make it to bed. She woke, ravenous, only to find Tony had risen before her. When she made her way to the kitchen, she found him dressed and standing in front of the coffee press. He had showered and shaved and looked more like his old self, less bent and drawn. She moved in behind him and wrapped her arms around him. “You’re looking better this morning,” she said.

“I’m fine.” He filled a mug from the press, then pulled a second mug from a hook beneath the cabinet, filled it and handed it to her. “When are you going back to Iowa?” he asked.

The suddenness of the question startled her. She sipped her coffee and studied him over the rim of the mug, trying to gauge his mood. He stared down into his own cup, his expression sullen. “You sound like you’re anxious for me to go,” she said.

“You’re not finding out anything about your sister here,” he said. “I know you have a job and a home and friends there.”

She set her unfinished coffee on the counter. “Do you want me to leave?”

He shrugged. “If you’re going to go anyway, you might as well leave now.”

Last night he had clung to her as if he never wanted to let go. Now he was practically pushing her out the door. “I don’t understand you,” she said. “I thought you liked me. I thought we were good together.” She almost said she was thinking about staying in Eagle Mountain. Because of him. But she had too much pride to let him know how much he was hurting her.

"I don't do long relationships." He looked at her then, his expression bleak. "That's just how I am."

"Who says?"

"I say."

He didn't do long relationships—with her. That was all she heard, the words making pain bloom somewhere mid-sternum. No wonder people who knew nothing about anatomy talked about heartache as a physical illness.

But as much as she was hurting, she was also furious. How dare he make her care so much, then toss her away. She wanted to tell him as much—to scream that he was a horrible person for treating her this way. But when she opened her mouth, all that came out was an anguished cry. Tears flooding her eyes, she turned and ran from the house.

She started the car and, shaking all over, sped out of Tony's driveway. When she reached the turn onto the road, she stopped and forced herself to calm down. The last thing she wanted was to wreck her car. She half laughed, half sobbed at the idea. She would be hurt in a ditch, and the call would go out to SAR and Tony would have to come and rescue her.

She kept her speed down and forced herself to pay attention as she drove. Focusing on driving was a good way to keep her emotions under control, though she had a knot of tears in the back of her throat, waiting to burst forth as soon as she was alone.

She turned onto the main highway leading to town and was starting to relax a little more when a blaring horn sent a jolt of panic through her. She stomped on the brakes and looked around, in time to see a pickup truck come up on her right, so close her car shook as it roared past, horn blasting. She tried to see who was driving but could make out nothing through the tinted windows. Before she could remember to note the license plate, the vehicle was gone.

Shaking, she pulled her car to the shoulder and sat, gripping the steering wheel so tightly her fingers ached. Her fantasy of having Tony come to rescue her didn't seem so far-fetched now. What was up with that driver? Was he just a jerk, or had he been trying to frighten her?

After a few minutes, she felt calm enough to proceed and drove the rest of the way to the inn. She managed to get to her room without being seen and sank onto her bed. But she didn't collapse, sobbing. She thought about Tony and about the reckless driver who had frightened her. And she thought about Liz and her failure to find anything that pointed to her sister's killer.

Maybe Tony was right. Maybe it was time for her to give up and go home.

Chapter Seventeen

Tony threw himself into physical therapy. When he wasn't at the therapist's office or the gym, he was working, surveying for a state-road project near Eagle Mountain. His goal every day was to fall into bed so tired he didn't have time to think about Kelsey. He avoided going by the Alpiner Inn or anywhere in town where he might run into her.

But he couldn't avoid thoughts of Kelsey altogether. Three days after she had rushed out of his house, the article about her search for her sister's killer was the front-page story in the *Eagle Mountain Examiner.* Tony stared for a long time at the photo of Kelsey that accompanied the article. She stood outside the Alpiner, looking into the camera with a serious, determined expression. Did others looking at this photo recognize the sadness in her eyes? Could they understand how losing her sister had meant losing the rest of her family as well?

Woman Searches for Sister's Killer

Kelsey Chapman came to Eagle Mountain because of family. Not the family who lives here, but the family who died here. Kelsey's sister, Elizabeth Chapman, was killed in April, more than two decades ago, and her murderer has never been found. Kelsey has been trying to uncover new information that might lead law enforcement to her sister's killer.

"All I know is that Liz came to Eagle Mountain to be with a man she met online," Kelsey, an accountant in her home of Mount Vernon, Iowa, says. "I was only eight years old at the time. Liz was eighteen, but I remember her talking about the man, whom she called Mountain Man. We never knew his name."

Sheriff Travis Walker says the case remains open, but law enforcement has few clues to go on. "Ms. Chapman gave school authorities a false address and led people to believe she lived alone," he says. "No one has been able to identify the man she supposedly came here to be with, and we haven't found a match for the DNA evidence collected at the crime scene."

Elizabeth Chapman's body was found

near Kestrel Trail by Tony Meisner, who was a teenager at the time. A classmate of Liz's, he recognized the body and ran to notify the sheriff's department.

"I believe Liz was killed by someone she knew," Kelsey says. "Someone she went hiking with that day, or someone she met up with on the trail. If anyone remembers seeing Liz with a man—either on the trail or at any other time—please get in touch with me or with the sheriff. That person might not be her killer, but it would be one more lead we could follow up on."

"We're happy to investigate any new information in the case," Sheriff Walker says.

Kelsey knows she will have to return to Iowa soon, maybe without answers to her sister's murder. "It's been good for me, being here," she says. "I feel like I understand what Liz loved about this place, and I've met people who remember her and what she was like then. It's made me feel closer to her, but nothing would be as good as knowing what really happened to her. I would really like that kind of closure."

Tony hurled the paper across the room. Of course, he had known Kelsey would leave soon, but seeing it confirmed in black and white made the pain worse. He ground the base of his palms into his eyes, then straightened and retrieved the paper. He smoothed it out and folded it so that Kelsey's picture was faceup. She smiled back at him. One more thing he wanted and couldn't have.

The text message alert from his phone pulled him from his misery, and he thumbed to a message from Search and Rescue. A semitruck had gone off the side of Dixon Pass. Driver alive and responsive, the message read.

Tony was relieved to have something to focus on besides himself. He arrived at SAR headquarters to find a full contingent of volunteers assembled, including Ted. "I was here reading through the archives for my book when the call came in," Ted said. "That driver is one lucky son of a gun. That area where he went off is a deadly sharp curve."

Sheri decided that she, Ryan and Danny would climb down to the driver, who had been able to shout a response to the tourist who had first noticed the fresh skid marks headed into the canyon. The tourist had seen the headlights of the big truck shining up from below and called in the incident. "Tony, I want you as incident commander up top," Sheri instructed.

"Happy to do it," Tony said. There was a time he would have been one of the primary climbers on a descent like this, but he knew he wasn't up to that today. Sheri probably knew it, too, but didn't feel the need to point it out. He could still be useful managing the mission. He moved to help Ryan and Eldon collect the gear they would need. Ted joined them.

"I saw the article in the paper about Kelsey," Ted said.

Tony didn't reply. He didn't want to talk about Kelsey.

"Sounds like she'll be going back to Iowa soon," Ted said.

"I guess so." Tony grabbed another climbing helmet and shoved it into a duffel.

"It's just as well," Ted said. "She was just stirring up everybody. Whoever killed that girl is long gone."

"What do you know about it, Ted?" Ryan asked.

A red flush darkened Ted's neck and cheeks. "I don't know anything," he barked. "I didn't even know the girl. I'm just saying that stuff like that article in the paper upsets people for no reason. They start thinking this is a dangerous place and looking at guys like they might be murderers or something."

"Her sister was murdered," Tony said. "She has a right to try to find out who did it." He slung the duffel over his shoulder and headed for the Beast. It was either that or punch Ted. Usually, he tolerated the older man's pontificating, but he didn't have the patience for it today.

The sheriff's department had closed the road up the pass to one lane of traffic a quarter mile before the place where the 18-wheeler had gone off the side. Flashing lights from several sheriff's department SUVs and an ambulance that had gotten to the scene ahead of Search and Rescue were visible a mile up the canyon.

"Looks like he took the curve here too sharp and the back wheels of the trailer went off the edge," Deputy Wes Landry said as the volunteers gathered around him for a status report. "The cargo in the trailer may have shifted and pulled him right down."

"That's a seventy-foot drop, easy," Tony said. "And straight down."

"You're sure the driver's alive?" Sheri asked.

"He shouted up that he's okay, just trapped in the driver's compartment."

Sheri took out a battery-operated hailer and went to the edge of the canyon. The others ranged along the rim, looking down at a truck, which more closely resembled a wad of tinfoil. Shredded cardboard littered the canyon like confetti, and miscellaneous bits of metal that might have been part of the cargo hung from tree limbs and draped across boulders. "This is Eagle Mountain Search and Rescue," Sheri called. "We're coming down to get you."

"Great!" came the clear response. "Be careful. I'm not going anywhere."

"He must be in pretty good shape," Ryan said. "He's kept his sense of humor."

Within minutes, the team had established anchors and begun the descent. Tony monitored the situation from above while the EMTs sat on the bumper of the ambulance and waited. The day was crisp but sunny, warm enough that Tony soon shed his jacket.

"How are you doing, Tony?" Hannah, on duty as a paramedic with the ambulance crew, came to stand beside him.

"I'm okay," he said. He focused on the climbers descending to the truck, but he could feel Hannah watching him.

"I was a little worried when you weren't at the meeting Friday night," she said. "Ted said he thought you were pretty banged up after that call on Mount Baker."

Ted always had an opinion, whether it was backed by fact or not. "I'm fine," Tony said again.

"That was a good article in the paper about Kelsey and her sister," Hannah said. "I hope it brings some new leads in the case."

"She hasn't had any luck turning up any new information so far," Tony said.

"Still, there are a lot of people in town who were here back when Liz was killed," Hannah said. "Someone must have seen or heard something, even if they didn't think it was important at the time. I asked Ted about it, and he said he never even heard of Liz Chapman until he responded to the call about her body."

"Ted was a lot older than Liz," Tony said. "No reason he would know her."

"She was really pretty," Hannah said. "I thought he might have remembered her for that reason alone. He can be a bit of a flirt, you know."

Tony stared at her. "Are we talking about the same Ted?"

Hannah laughed. "I know. But I remember when I first joined SAR, he went out of his way to be friendly to me. It wasn't sleazy or anything, but it was definitely flirty." She shrugged. "I just figured he was one of those older guys who thinks he's irresistible to all women."

Tony's radio crackled and Sheri said, "We're here and the truck is a wreck, but the driver's compartment somehow survived pretty much intact. As soon as we pry open the passenger door, we'll have him out. He says he's got a banged-up shoulder and a bump on his head, but he swears there's no blood and he sounds coherent and calm."

"Good news," Tony said. "Do you need the Jaws?" The hydraulic extractor, otherwise known as the Jaws of Life, could open up vehicles to allow access to an injured person inside.

"Ryan thinks he can pop the door with a pry bar," Sheri said. "I'll let you know if we need anything else."

Hannah returned to the ambulance, and Tony monitored the situation with Sheri. Ten minutes later, the driver was out of the cab of the truck, standing upright and telling everyone he could walk up under his own power. Danny examined him, said he should probably get his head injury checked out—just to be safe—then persuaded him to allow Search and Rescue to haul him up the cliff in a litter. When the driver balked, Sheri pointed out the only alternative was to climb straight up under his own power. With no previous climbing experience and an admitted fear of heights, the driver opted to be strapped onto the litter and hauled up with a volunteer on either side to steady his ascent.

Cheers rose from the gathered emergency personnel when the litter tipped over the edge of the canyon and volunteers rushed forward to free the driver, who stood shakily and thanked everyone in sight. Hannah escorted him to the ambulance for a ride to the hospital while the others gathered their gear and prepared to return to headquarters.

It wasn't until they were unloading at headquarters that Tony remembered Hannah's words. "Sheri, what did you think of Ted when you first joined Search and Rescue?" he asked.

"Everyone said he was the most experienced volunteer," she said. "Someone who had served in every capacity, and who knew the terrain around here better than anyone."

"Right. But what did you think of him personally?"

Sheri frowned at him. "Why are you asking?"

"Hannah said Ted flirted with her a lot when she first joined," Tony said. "I wondered if he did that with all the women."

Sheri nodded. "Oh, yeah. Ted thinks he's quite the ladies' man." She shrugged. "I thought he was harmless. Way too old for me."

"Huh. I never noticed."

"Well, you wouldn't! He wouldn't have flirted with you, and he wasn't annoying about it. I told him flat-out I wasn't interested, and he backed off." She stowed a splint in a plastic bin and snapped on the lid, then turned to him. "Has someone complained about Ted? Said he was harassing them?"

Tony shook his head. "Nothing like that."

"Good. Because I never saw anything like that. He's just one of those men who flirt with women—especially younger women. To tell you the truth, I thought he was probably just lonely." She picked up the bin and carried it to the closet.

Tony felt a twinge of sympathy for Ted. Despite his bragging about being a ladies' man, Ted hadn't had a steady relationship that Tony knew about in all the time they had known each other. Neither had Tony, so he knew a few things about loneliness. And he had always looked up to Ted, who had taken the younger man under his wing and taught Tony most of what he knew about search and rescue work. He had sympathized with Ted's loss of physical prowess as he aged, which had forced his retirement from SAR, and had been happy that his mentor had found a new role with the organization as the group's historian.

But knowing Ted had hit on younger women was a little unsettling. If he was so interested in younger women, how had he failed to notice Liz Chapman—a new young woman in a small town where newcomers stood out? Was Ted telling the truth when he said he didn't know Liz, or was he lying to avoid having others look at him with suspicion, the way they had looked at Tony?

Tony knew there were still people who suspected him of having been involved in Liz's death. He had known her. He was known to have a crush on her. And he was the person who found her body. He supposed all of that looked suspicious.

But Kelsey had believed he was innocent.

Hadn't she?

KELSEY THOUGHT ABOUT sending the article from the *Eagle Mountain Examiner* to her mother, but why bother? Apparently, Mary had changed her mind about wanting to know anything about her elder daughter. She didn't want to "dig Liz up again." But Kelsey had never buried her sister. Liz lived on as the smiling, pretty teen who had snuggled with her and laughed with her and promised to see her again soon.

"Kelsey!" Brit flagged her down when she returned to the inn Wednesday afternoon, after another day searching the newspaper archives for any previous mention she might have missed that could related to Liz's case. Kelsey waited for Brit to catch up with her. "That was a good article in the paper yesterday," Brit said. "I hope it yields some results for the investigation."

"I hope so, too," Kelsey said. So far, no one had contacted her, but maybe the sheriff's department had heard something.

"Do you want to extend your stay again?"

Brit asked. "We have you booked through Friday, and I'm not trying to run you off. We'd love to have you continue to stay with us. But I need to know sooner rather than later. It's getting to be our busy season and we have lots of calls for bookings."

Last week, she had been certain she would stay in Eagle Mountain, even relocate here. But that had been when she thought she and Tony had a future together. "I plan to leave, unless something turns up," she said. "I promise I'll let you know as soon as possible if I do end up staying, and I understand if you don't have anything available."

Brit patted Kelsey's arm. "We really would love to have you stay. It's been wonderful getting to know you."

Kelsey swallowed past a knot in her throat. Brit was so cheerful and kind—the way she remembered her own mother being before Liz had left them.

Brit turned to go, then turned back. "I almost forgot. I have a note for you at the front desk."

Kelsey's heart sped up. "Who is the note from?" Would Tony send a note? Why wouldn't he text or call or just stop by? She followed Brit to the front desk.

"I don't know." Brit retrieved an envelope from a drawer. "Someone dropped it through the mail slot. It was here when I came down this morning." She handed the envelope to Kelsey.

Kelsey studied her name on the front of the message. This wasn't Tony's precise script. And she didn't recognize the writing as belonging to anyone else she knew. She took the stairs to her room and waited until she was inside before she teased up the flap of the envelope. The message was typed on a half sheet of white paper: "I know some things I never told the cops about your sister because I was too afraid. But I want to tell you," she read. "Please meet me at six p.m. Wednesday at the trailhead for Kestrel Trail. There's something I need to show you."

She read the message over again. Was this for real or some cruel prank? If this had happened a few days ago, she would have asked Tony to go with her, but she couldn't do that now.

Should she tell the sheriff? Or would he think she was wasting his time? She punched in the number for the sheriff's department. Adelaide Kinkaid would know what she should do.

But instead of Adelaide, a different woman answered the phone. "Rayford County Sheriff," she said, her voice brisk.

"Is Adelaide there?" Kelsey asked.

"Ms. Kinkaid is away from the office today. How may I help you?"

"May I speak to the sheriff?"

"Sheriff Walker isn't available at the moment. What does this concern?"

Kelsey hung up. She didn't want to have to recap her whole story to a stranger. She read the note again. It was already after five. While the trail itself was fairly isolated, the trailhead was on a major road, and there were several trails branching off from it. Someone else would probably be there. And she had to find out who had written the note and what that person wanted to tell—and show—her about her sister.

She grabbed her backpack and keys and headed back downstairs. "Goodbye!" Brit called as Kelsey passed.

Kelsey waved but kept moving. She would have to hurry or she would be late. She didn't want to miss this opportunity.

Chapter Eighteen

"Set the stake right there, Ben." While his assistant hammered in the numbered stake marking the right-of-way for the new road project, Tony recorded the GPS coordinates and prepared to pack up his equipment.

"I hear that nephew of yours is doing a good job," Ben said when he had the stake in. He straightened and came to stand beside Tony. "Curtis says he'll be ready to go out in the field on his own next week, so you might be getting a new assistant."

"I don't know if I want to live *and* work with him," Tony said.

"Hey, it's a great excuse for you to boss him around," Ben said. "And really, he's a good kid. We had a beer after work the other day, and he sure thinks the world of you."

"Yeah, well, I think the world of him, too." Chris knew that, didn't he?

The growl of a pickup truck engine made

him look up in time to see Ted race by in his battered vehicle. Tony lifted a hand in a wave but Ted, hunched over the steering wheel, never looked up.

"Sounds like Ted has an exhaust leak in his truck," Ben said as he approached, tripod over one shoulder. "He ought to have that looked at."

Tony nodded, something else about the way the truck sounded in the back of his mind, but he couldn't quite retrieve the thought. He and Ben finished loading their gear and were just climbing into Tony's truck when his phone message alert went off. Tony checked the screen. "Is it a search and rescue call?" Ben asked.

Tony nodded. "Lost fisherman up at Crystal Lake."

Ben made a sucking sound with his teeth. "Bet he went through the ice. This time of year, there's always somebody who thinks it will hold. The county ought to just post signs telling people to stay off the ice after April 1. It might look solid, but there's just too much warm weather these days, even in the high country."

Tony nodded absently, not really listening as Ben continued with a story about a friend of his who went through the ice crossing a pond somewhere south of town. His attention was divided between thoughts of what they needed to prepare for the rescue—and possible body retrieval—of the fisherman and wondering where Ted had been going in such a hurry.

He dropped Ben at his truck at the surveying office, then headed to SAR headquarters. Most of the other volunteers were assembled, loading the Beast with the equipment they might need, from supplemental oxygen to waders and an inflatable rubber raft.

"We're waiting on Anna and Jacquie," Sheri said when Tony approached. "Jacquie hasn't been certified for water searches yet, but Anna has been training her and I think she's our best chance of finding this guy if he went in."

"You think we're searching for a body?" Tony asked.

Sheri nodded. "His brother and his son were with him and they searched for an hour before they called us."

She looked around at the crowd of volunteers. "Have you seen Ted?" she asked.

"I saw him right before I left to come here," Tony said. "He was in his truck, racing somewhere. After I got the call, I thought he might have been headed here."

Sheri shook her head. "No, and I'm more annoyed with him than usual. He was supposed to meet me here an hour ago to help with a grant application I'm working on. He has all the statistics on the number of rescues we've done in the past two years, miles logged and things like that I need for the application. Which direction was he headed?"

"South," Tony said. Not toward SAR headquarters, come to think of it.

"Crystal Lake is east, so he wasn't headed there." She shrugged. "Maybe he forgot."

Danny joined them in time to hear this last statement. "Are you talking about Ted?" he asked.

"Yes," Sheri said. "He flaked out on helping me with the grant application this afternoon."

"He's been acting strange lately," Danny said.

"Stranger than usual?" Sheri asked.

"He's always been a grouch, but yesterday he flew off the handle when I asked him if he'd seen the new issue of the *Examiner*," Danny said. "There was an ad in there for some Rossignol powder skis, and I knew he used to have that model and I wanted to know what he thought of them. But I never got around to asking him because he went on this rant about how he didn't have time to sit around reading the paper and all they printed was garbage anyway."

"Sometimes behavior changes like that are linked to something physical," Sheri said. "Maybe it's time someone suggested he see a doctor." She turned to Tony. "You've known him longer than any of us. Maybe you could bring it up."

"I can try," Tony said. "But I doubt he'll take the suggestion well." Something was definitely up with Ted lately. He struck Tony as someone with a lot on his mind—but what had him so upset?

KELSEY SLOWED TO turn into the parking lot for the starting point for Kestrel Trail but hesitated when she saw that the only other vehicle there was an older model pickup truck. She flashed back to the headlights from the vehicle that had almost run her and Tony down the other night. Tony had said he thought that had been a truck. And a truck had come up behind her the other day, blaring its horn. But as she debated turning around and leaving, a familiar figure emerged from the vehicle and waved.

She relaxed as she recognized Ted, and then her heart began to beat faster—not with fear but with excitement. He had lived here when Liz was killed. He had been standing outside the ice-cream parlor the night her friends said she was meeting someone. Had he remembered the one thing that would help her find Liz's murderer?

She pulled in next to Ted and got out of her car. "Thanks for meeting me out here," he said.

"I wanted someplace where we could talk privately, without worrying about anyone overhearing."

"Your note said you knew something about Liz," she said. "What is it?"

"I did see her with someone outside the ice-cream shop that night." He shoved both hands in the pockets of his jeans. "I kept quiet because the person I saw is a good friend of mine," he said. "I couldn't believe he would do anything to hurt your sister, but now I think maybe I was wrong."

Kelsey curled her hands into fists, trying to keep them from shaking. She had waited for this so long. "Who did you see with Liz that night?" she asked, fighting to keep her voice steady.

He stared at the ground between them for a long moment. She fought the urge to shake him. To demand he tell her the truth he had been hiding all these years. But she forced herself to wait. When Ted finally looked up at her, his expression was mournful. "It was Tony," he said. "I know you don't want to hear this, but I think he's the one who killed your sister."

THE SEARCH AND Rescue team waited on the shores of Crystal Lake while Anna Trent and her search dog, a black standard poodle named Jacquie, trailed around the shoreline. Jacquie snuffled through the tall rushes around the dam inlet, then hurried down to the water, pulling Anna after her. The fisherman, Mike Munro, had come to the lake with his brother and son, who waited on a rise above the rescuers, with other friends and family members who had come to offer what support they could. A long half hour into the search, Anna raised her hand and called out, "I see something under the ice."

While Jacquie stood at attention on the shore, focused on the flash of red beneath the shelf of ice, Eldon, Tony and Danny took turns chopping at the frozen surface with an ax until they had cleared a space large enough to reach in with a grappling hook and snag Mike Munro's red fleece jacket. Mike's brother moved forward to confirm the identification, and they solemnly slid the body into an opaque black bag and carried it to the waiting ambulance, which would transport it to the morgue in the basement of the hospital.

A subdued group returned to Search and Rescue headquarters. Everything had gone off smoothly, exactly as it should have. The fisherman had probably died within minutes of going into the cold water, and there was nothing the group could have done to save him, but coming back without a live body never felt good.

The rescue over, Tony's thoughts shifted

back to Ted. Too many things about the way his friend had been acting lately bothered him. Why was Ted so interested in Kelsey, constantly asking about her, yet disparaging her search for her sister?

The need to talk to Kelsey overwhelmed him. Why had he been so standoffish, staying away from her? He needed to apologize for being such a fool. Even if she hated him for treating her the way he had, he needed to make sure she was all right.

He left SAR headquarters and drove to the Alpiner. Brit looked up from behind the front desk when he entered. "Is Kelsey here?" he asked before Brit could even say hello.

"I'm sorry, Tony, she isn't. She left a couple of hours ago."

He grabbed hold of the front desk to steady himself and silently swore. He was too late. Kelsey had gone back to Iowa. She hadn't even bothered to say goodbye. But why should she? He hadn't given her any reason to think he was still her friend. Her lover. Though he wanted to be that, and so much more.

Maybe it wasn't too late. "Do you have an address for her in Iowa?" he asked.

Brit frowned. "I might have. But why do you need her address in Iowa?"

"If she's gone back there, I thought I might

write her." Did that sound pathetic? Did people even write letters anymore?

Brit was still staring at him, confusion on her face. "Never mind," he said. "I'll call her." That's what he should do. He had her number.

"Oh my goodness, I just realized what you're thinking," Brit said. "Kelsey hasn't gone back to Iowa. Not yet, anyway. She just went out."

"Where did she go?" Maybe he could find her and try to explain himself in person.

"I think she might have gone hiking. She had her day pack with her."

"Hiking where?"

Brit shook her head. "I don't know. She didn't say."

He remembered again seeing Ted, driving out of town. Away from SAR headquarters. Away from Crystal Lake.

Toward the trailhead for Kestrel Trail. Suddenly, he was certain that was where Ted had been going. Where Kelsey had headed, as well. He might be wrong, but he couldn't ignore this instinct that told him he was right.

Hand shaking, he pulled out his phone and punched in Kelsey's number. It rang and rang before going to voice mail. "This is Tony. I'm sorry I've been so foolish. Please call me. I need to know you're okay."

Fear clawing at his chest, he called Ted. No

answer. He didn't bother leaving a message. Instead, he thought about the sound of Ted's truck. Ben thought the truck had an exhaust leak. It was the same sound the truck that had tried to run them down weeks ago made.

Ted had denied knowing Liz, but how could he have not at least been aware of her? She was an attractive newcomer, at a time when newcomers were rare enough to draw a lot of attention. Ted had been standing on the sidewalk near the ice-cream parlor on the night she had told her friends she was meeting someone. He said he stepped out for a smoke, but back then, people still smoked in bars. There was no reason for Ted to stand outside that night unless he was waiting for someone.

Unless he was waiting for Liz.

Tony called the sheriff. Not the emergency number, but Travis's personal cell. "Is something wrong, Tony?" Travis asked by way of greeting.

"I'm not positive, but I think Kelsey Chapman is in trouble," he said. "I think she's with Ted Carruthers, and I think he might intend to hurt her."

He waited for Travis to ask him what proof he had to back his suspicions, but the sheriff did not. "Where are they now?" he asked.

"I'm not positive, but my best guess is that

they're at Kestrel Trail." It was where Liz had died. Would Ted think there was some kind of symmetry in ending up there again after all these years?

"I'll send someone to check it out," Travis said.

Tony ended the call, grateful the sheriff was a man of few words. But Tony wasn't going to wait for a deputy to show up. Kelsey had been gone at least two hours now. More than enough time for Ted to harm her, if that was what he intended. Long years in rescue work had taught Tony that even a few minutes could make a difference when it came to saving someone. He had to hurry, before it was too late.

KELSEY STARED, sure she had heard Ted incorrectly. "Tony?" she gasped.

Expression still glum, Ted nodded. "I'm sorry," he said. "All these years, I've tried to put it out of my mind, to tell myself what I saw was innocent. But the other day I was up on this trail, near where Liz died." He pointed to the trail head. "And I saw something there that proved to me that Tony was the only one who could have killed your sister."

"I don't understand." She shook her head. Not Tony. Not the man who had been such a friend to her. Such a gentle lover. "Why would Tony have killed Liz?"

"Tony had a crush on Liz. A crush she didn't reciprocate. I think he invited her to go hiking with him that day and when they got to that rocky bench with the great view, he told her how he felt about her. Maybe she said something to hurt his feelings. Maybe she laughed. You women don't understand what something like that can do to a guy. There he was, pouring out his heart to her, and she acted like it didn't mean anything. That kind of rejection really messes with a man's head. It can make him do things he wouldn't ordinarily do."

Was Ted still talking about Tony? "Tony isn't like that," she said.

"Anyone could have done what he did, in that position," Ted said. "He snapped and killed her. Then he ran away. But his conscience wouldn't let him just leave her there, so when no one found her after a week, he played the hero and 'found' her body himself."

"I can't believe it." The words came out just above a whisper, though inside, Kelsey was shouting. *Not Tony!*

"It makes sense if you think about it," Ted said. "Tony has always been a little odd. Standoffish. He doesn't make friends easily, isn't one to socialize a lot. He's the kind of man who probably has a lot of secrets."

Those things don't make a person a killer, Kelsey wanted to say, but she couldn't force the words past the knot of fear in her throat. Tony had admitted to having a crush on Liz. And he had been the one to find her body. The sheriff's department had even suspected him of having killed her. "His DNA doesn't match what the sheriff's department collected from underneath Liz's fingernails," she said. "They tested Tony at the time."

"Maybe they made a mistake when they collected it," Ted said. "Or maybe that DNA is from someone who shook hands with her earlier in the day. We all know that so-called evidence can lie."

But could DNA evidence lie? She stared at Ted. "I'm having a hard time digesting all this."

He nodded. "It's a lot to take in. And I might have kept quiet longer. After all, Tony is like a son to me in some ways. I've been watching him, and I don't think he's ever hurt anyone else. Telling everyone about this won't bring your sister back."

"But you can't let a murderer go free!"

"I guess that's true." He stared off to the side, as if seeing something she couldn't see. "There's another reason I decided I had to tell you," he said. His gaze met hers again—mournful eyes set in a weathered face. "I saw how close Tony was getting to you—how much time the two of you were spending together. I knew you had to go back to Iowa soon and I worried that he might not take it well. He might do to you the same thing he did to your sister. You and Liz are a lot alike, you know. At least, from the pictures I've seen."

Kelsey put a hand to her head, as if to quell the dizziness his words sent washing over her. She couldn't believe Tony would ever hurt her. Would he?

"Hike up the trail with me a little ways, and I'll show you what I found," Ted said. "You'll want to show the sheriff. It pretty much proves Tony is the one who killed Liz." He motioned that she should go ahead of him.

Numb, she started up the trail, Ted close behind her. He didn't say anything, and she was grateful that he didn't try to engage her in further conversation. Thoughts tumbled in her head like gravel in a rushing stream. Was she such a poor judge of character that she had fallen for her sister's killer? She hugged her arms across her stomach, cold all over.

She walked slowly, as if her feet were reluctant to reach this supposed proof that the man she trusted—a man she had fallen in love with—was a murderer. Every step was an effort, but she forced herself to keep moving. After an hour they were at the place in the trail where Tony had taken her when they hiked together—the location where he said he had found Liz's body. She stared at the gray rock and bunches of green grass and short yellow wildflowers sprouting up around it. "If Tony killed Liz because she rejected him, who was Mountain Man?" she asked. "Who was the older man who persuaded her to come live with him in Eagle Mountain?"

Ted frowned. "Liz must have made him up."

"But she didn't," Kelsey said. "The sheriff has printouts between Liz and Mountain Man, and his messages originated in Eagle Mountain. And he sent her a bus ticket to come here. Liz never could have done that on her own."

"It sounds to me as if she could have done anything she put her mind to," he said. "She was that sure of herself, coming here by herself and even fooling the school the way she did."

Liz was stubborn. Impulsive. Strong-willed. But Kelsey had found no evidence that she was a liar. "What is it you wanted to show me?" she asked, impatient to be away from here. Alone, where she could think.

"It's right over here." He stepped up on the

largest rock and held his hand out for her. "Come up and I'll show you."

She rejected his offer to help and hopped up on the rock beside him. "Where is it?"

"It's just behind there." He pointed toward the ground beside another boulder. "Do you see?"

She bent and stared at the ground. "I don't see anything. What—"

But she never finished the sentence. Piercing pain exploded in the back of her head, and everything went black.

TONY BROKE EVERY speed limit on the drive to the trailhead, praying as he gripped the steering wheel and kept his foot on the gas pedal that his instincts were wrong. But he spotted Ted's truck when he was still fifty yards from the parking area, and as he turned in, he caught sight of Kelsey's car parked beside it. He skidded to a stop, cut the engine and leapt out, racing up the steep trail. He ran, not as if his own life depended on speed but as if the life of the one person who mattered most to him was on the line.

His legs usually hurt when he tried to run, but today he felt nothing but the icy fear in the pit of his stomach as he pounded up the trail. With no pack or oxygen tank or awkward medical gear to carry, he covered ground quickly. As he topped each rise he stared ahead, expecting to see Ted, or Kelsey or—worst of all—both of them together. But only wildflowers and rocks and blue sky met his gaze.

Then he spotted movement far ahead. Two figures on the rocks. He picked up his pace, every part of him aching now, sharp pains in his legs, dull throbbing in his chest, a prickly sensation across his palms. He clenched and unclenched his fingers. Why hadn't he thought to bring a weapon? And what would he have brought? A kitchen knife? A scalpel?

"Stop right there, Tony!"

Ted's voice boomed out across the empty landscape. Tony stumbled in mid-stride, and had to pull back to catch himself. He stared up the slope, at Ted, who held Kelsey's limp body in his arms. "What did you do to her?" he shouted, his voice breaking with rage.

"I told her the truth." Ted shook his head. "Or a version of it. I told her how you murdered her sister because she didn't love you the way you loved her."

"But you murdered Liz," Tony said.

"She was supposed to stay with me for the rest of her life," Ted said. "That's why I sent her the bus ticket. Why I helped her lie to the school district. But she changed her mind. She told me she wanted to go home. She wanted to leave me.

Do you know what it feels like to have someone you love abandon you that way?"

Tony stared, not at Ted but at Kelsey. She lay back in Ted's arms, head limp, eyes half-closed, mouth partly open.

"I couldn't let her leave me," Ted said. "She was all I ever wanted. I was good to her. Why wasn't that enough?"

Tony shifted his gaze back to his longtime friend and mentor. Ted didn't look good. His skin was gray, his face deeply lined. "And you killed her for that?" Tony asked.

Ted looked down at Kelsey, and Tony wondered if he was seeing Liz there instead. "It was an accident," Ted said, his voice gentle. "I tried to move in closer, to kiss her and tell her we would find a way to work things out. She pushed me, so I pushed her back." He shook his head. "I only meant to grab her, to make her listen to sense, but she struggled so much. The more she struggled, the tighter I held her. And then she just…died. So in the end, she left me anyway."

"Why didn't you call for help?" Tony asked.

"It was too late. No one could have saved her."

"The medical examiner said she was strangled," Tony said.

Ted jerked his head up. "He's a liar," he said,

his voice a harsh growl. "They're all liars." He shaped his hand to Kelsey's throat. His fingers wrapped around it easily. Dizziness and fear rocked Tony back on his heels. He took three steps forward while Ted was so focused on Kelsey. "You have to be very careful with people's necks," Ted said. "They're very delicate."

A chill shuddered through Tony as he remembered how Ted had said those very words in the CPR classes he taught every spring and fall at the fire house. They had never sounded so sinister before. He swallowed and tried to keep his voice calm. "You're right," he said. "Necks are very sensitive. Why don't you lay Kelsey down and I'll check hers for you?"

Ted jerked his gaze away from Kelsey again. "Don't move," he ordered.

Kelsey moaned, and they both stared. She rolled her head from side to side, grimacing. "Now look what you did," Ted said. "You woke her." He hefted her higher, though he had to move his hand away from her throat to do so.

Tony searched the ground for a weapon. Rocks were a natural choice, but any with the size and heft to do damage were too far away to be of any use to him. All he had were words, and he had never been good with those. But he had to try. "The sheriff is on his way," he said.

"I told him I suspected you killed Liz and that you might try to hurt Kelsey."

The lines on Ted's forehead and around his eyes deepened. "You shouldn't have done that," he said. He looked out past Tony's shoulder. "But it doesn't matter. They won't get here in time."

In time for what? Tony wanted to ask but didn't. Instead, he asked, "What are you going to do?"

"I'm going to kill Kelsey, then kill you," Ted said, in a voice someone might use to describe their morning workout. "When the sheriff does arrive, I'll tell him how I found you both—a murder-suicide I was too late to stop."

"Travis isn't a fool," Tony said. "He won't take your word for it. He'll want proof."

Ted shrugged. "Maybe I'll scrape Liz's hand across your face and collect some DNA for them to find," he said. "That should make them happy."

He had said Liz, not Kelsey. Did Ted even know where he was and who he was with right now? Or was he twenty years in the past, with another young woman who had rejected him? Tony didn't have any more time for questions like that one. He had to act. Ted's hand tightened around Kelsey's throat, and she groaned louder.

Tony ran—not away but straight toward Ted and Kelsey. He hit with all the force he could muster, trying to aim the brunt of the impact at Ted but unable to avoid Kelsey, who was crushed between them. The two men each struggled to hold on to her. Though Ted was older, he was still strong and refused to let go. Furious and frustrated, Tony leaned down and bit the older man, hard, on the wrist.

With a wounded yowl, Ted released his hold. Kelsey tumbled to the ground and Tony punched Ted in the jaw, knocking him backward, but Ted grabbed Tony's ankle and brought him down, too. The two men rolled and grappled, sharp rocks digging into Tony's back and shoulders. How close were they to the edge? The slope was steep enough here they would roll for a while if they tumbled over the edge of the bench.

Ted had him on his back now, trying to wrap his hands around Tony's throat as Tony grasped his wrists and tried to push him away. A rock with a knife edge dug into his back and his recently-knitted muscles and bones protested at this strain. He tried to shift beneath the older man, but Ted had him firmly pinned. Where was the deputy the sheriff had promised to send?

Maybe the deputy wasn't coming. Kelsey wasn't going to suddenly regain consciousness and pick up a rock and hurl it at Ted, either. Tony was on his own. He ought to be used to that by now.

With a howl of rage, he shoved up against Ted and rolled to his left, reversing their positions so that now he was on top and Ted on bottom. Then he brought his knee up and planted it firmly in Ted's stomach. He found the rock that had been digging into his back moments before and brought it down on Ted's forehead. Ted groaned, then fell silent, and Tony shoved to his feet, blood and tears dripping down his face.

He wiped his eyes to clear his vision, then staggered over to Kelsey. He knelt beside her, and gently touched her cheek. He ought to assess her, as he would any person in need he was called to rescue, but all he could do was stare. "Please wake up," he said, his voice choked with tears. "Please, please wake up."

Her eyes fluttered, and she looked up at him. "Tony," she whispered, before she closed her eyes again.

Tony tried to stand, but toppled to one side instead. He was trying again to get to his feet when Deputy Jake Gwynn and Sheriff Travis Walker came striding up the trail toward them. Travis stood over them. "What happened to you?" he asked.

"Ted killed Liz Chapman," Tony said. "And he tried to kill Kelsey. Then he was going to kill me and tell you I was the murderer."

"When I saw Ted's truck, I radioed for an ambulance," Travis said. "Just in case."

Tony nodded, then rested his forehead on his

upraised knees, too exhausted to say anything else. But he kept one hand on Kelsey, her pulse steady beneath his fingers. She was alive, and right now that was all he needed.

KELSEY'S HEAD HURT, and when she opened her eyes, the light made the pain worse. She closed her eyes again, but someone was shaking her. "Kelsey. Kelsey, you need to wake up."

She shook her head, but the voice persisted, telling her she had to wake up. She forced her eyes open again and stared up at a man she didn't recognize. "Who are you?" she asked. Except her throat was so dry the words came out as more moaning.

"I'm Dr. Harrison," the man said. "Do you remember what happened to you?"

She closed her eyes again, some of the fog lifting as she remembered Ted telling her those awful things about Tony.

"Kelsey, don't go away from us again. Open your eyes for me, please."

She opened her eyes. "I think Ted hit me," she said, the words clearer now. "Can I have some water?"

The doctor disappeared from view, but moments later returned and slipped a straw between her lips. She could only manage a couple of weak sips before he took it away. "You've sustained a concussion," he said. "You're in St. Joseph's Hospital in Junction. There's someone here who insists on seeing you."

The doctor left again, and was replaced by another, more welcome face. "Tony!" she said, and tried to smile, but the movement hurt too much.

"How are you feeling?" he asked.

"I've been better." She stared, taking in his bruised face. "What happened to you?"

He touched his bruised cheek and winced. "I was in a bit of a fight."

"Where's Ted?" she asked. "He told me some terrible things. He tried to say you...you..." She couldn't get the words out. They were too horrible.

"He lied," Tony said. "He lied to me and to everyone else. He killed Liz. He was Mountain Man. I'm sorry. I'm sorry about all of this. Mostly, I'm sorry I was so awful. I should have been a lot smarter. About Ted, but especially about you."

The doctor reappeared. "The sheriff is here," he said. "I told him he could have two minutes, then everyone has to leave this woman in peace."

Sheriff Walker loomed over her now. "Do you remember what happened?" he asked.

She nodded. "Ted asked me to meet him to tell me something he knew about Liz's killer. Then he hit me in the head." She winced. "I guess he tried to kill me, too." She didn't bother mentioning everything Ted had told her about Tony. That had to be all lies.

"We have Ted in custody," Travis said. "As soon as we're able we'll collect his DNA and compare it to the evidence we have from your sister, but we searched his home and we found this." He held out a small plastic bag with a white label stamped Evidence.

Kelsey put a hand to her throat and felt the small gold heart necklace there. The necklace's twin was in that bag. "That's Liz's," she said. "She gave me one just like it." She tugged at the chain until the heart was freed from the top of her hospital gown.

"We found a photo of your sister and some other things that point to Ted's involvement with her," Travis said. He tucked the bag with the necklace back into his pocket. "I'll get a full statement from you as soon as the doctor agrees."

"Time's up," the doctor said.

"We'll talk more later," Travis said, then left.

"Please, can I see Tony again?" Kelsey asked.

The doctor frowned and shook his head, but moments later, Tony was back in place. "I didn't believe him," she said before Tony could speak. "I didn't believe Ted when he told me you murdered Liz. I knew you wouldn't do something like that."

He took her hand in his and kissed her knuckles. "A lot of people would have believed him," he said.

"I'm not a lot of people." She took a deep breath. "And I'm in love with you. I have enough faith in myself to believe I wouldn't fall in love with a murderer."

He stilled, his hand still clutching her fingers. He stared into her eyes. "I love you, too," he said. "So much it scared me into pushing you away. Can you forgive me for that?"

"Yes. But don't let it happen again."

His smile was the warm, shy one that had made her catch her breath the very first time they met. As if even then her heart knew what her brain wasn't yet ready to accept. That all those other failed relationships and difficulties getting close to other people hadn't meant that she was too damaged to connect. She had only needed the right person to connect to. A man who understood what it was like to be alone from a young age. Someone like Tony, who was as afraid of pain as she was, but willing to take a risk. "Don't go back to Iowa," he said. "Stay here and give me a chance. Give us a chance."

She nodded. "I have to go back to settle things there, but I promise I'll come back here."

He patted her hand. "We'll find a way to make this work," he said, then left. She closed her eyes and drifted off. They would find a way, she was sure. They were two people who had made a habit now of doing the impossible.

Epilogue

Kelsey Chapman had never lived west of Mount Vernon, Iowa, when she steered her Honda Civic down the main street of Eagle Mountain, Colorado. She slowed the car to a crawl and almost stopped in the middle of the street as she stared up at the snow-covered mountains surrounding the town. She would always think of this place as the most beautiful spot in the world. Because of these mountains and that impossibly blue sky, and because of the friendships she had made here. The love she had found.

She drove on, through town to the A-frame cabin in the woods. She had barely turned into the drive when Tony emerged from the house and came to meet her. She shut off the engine and stepped out of the car and into his welcoming arms. "How was your trip?" he asked.

"Fine." They had talked every night while

she was away, so he already knew she had quit her job and given up her lease on her apartment.

The door to the house opened and Chris emerged—as tall and lanky as his uncle, his hair a darker shade of blond, his face clean-shaven. He grinned at Kelsey. "Don't worry," he said. "I'm only here to help with the heavy lifting." He nodded toward the rental trailer she towed behind her car. "I've got my own place now, so I won't be on the couch, cramping your style."

"It's a big change," Tony said, still watching her with concern.

"It's a good change." She patted his chest. "The Alpiner Inn has already hired me to do their accounts, and I'm sure I'll have other clients soon. Apparently, there's a real need for someone with my skills."

The worry left his eyes, replaced by warmth. "I have a real need for you," he said.

"Save it for later," Chris said. "Let's get this trailer unloaded."

They were bringing in the last of the boxes when a Rayford County Sheriff's Department SUV pulled into the drive. Sheriff Travis Walker stepped out and studied the trailer, then the trio in front of the house. "Hello, Kelsey," he said. "I heard you were arriving today."

"Hello, Sheriff," she said, wary.

Travis didn't keep them waiting long. "We got the DNA results back today," he said. "Ted is a match for what we collected from your sister."

Her shoulders sagged—with relief and sadness and so many emotions she couldn't untangle right now. Tony slipped his arm around her.

"Did you find any more of Liz's things?" she asked.

"Ted admitted he burned everything except the necklace," Travis said.

"Why did he insist on keeping their relationship secret?" Kelsey asked.

"Apparently, he had this fear that some other man would steal her away from him," Travis said. "He lied about his age in his emails because he worried she would hold that against him. Then, when she finally got to Eagle Mountain, he realized how many young, single men were in town compared to the number of single women. He was determined not to lose her."

"He was obsessed," she said.

Travis nodded. "For what it's worth, we don't think he killed anyone else. What happened with Liz apparently shook him enough he didn't risk it again—until you came along."

She shuddered, remembering those horrible moments beside Kestrel Trail. She still had headaches and dizzy spells from the concussion she had sustained, though her doctors assured her that would get better with time.

"The prosecutor will be in touch about the trial," Travis said. "In the meantime, welcome back." He nodded and returned to his vehicle.

Chris carried the last box into the house, then emerged, keys in hand. "I have to go," he said. "Good seeing you, Kelsey." He pulled on a helmet, then went to a motorcycle that had been parked beside the house.

Tony pulled her close again. "How did your mother take your leaving?"

Kelsey sighed. "She didn't have much of a reaction. She said, 'If that's what you really want to do,' then said she needed to go, she had a women's club meeting to attend. I think she spent so many years trying not to feel that she can't anymore."

"I almost made that mistake, until you came along," he said.

She stared into his eyes, so full of love and concern—and the doubts she shared. "Do you think we can do this?" she asked. "With our histories?"

He nodded. "We can do this. We both know how to do hard things. Good things." He kissed her, and the kiss made her believe him. She brought her hand up to cover the gold heart she wore around her neck. She was going to be happy here. The kind of happiness Liz would have wanted for her. The happiness she deserved.

* * * * *

Cindi Myers wraps up her miniseries
Eagle Mountain: Critical Response
next month with Secrets of Silverpeak Mine.

And look for the previous titles in the series:

Deception at Dixon Pass
Pursuit at Panther Point

Available now wherever Harlequin Intrigue books are sold!